# DUCKS
# IN DANGER

*Also from Avon Camelot by*
**Emily Costello**

ANIMAL EMERGENCY #1:
ABANDONED PUPPY

*Coming Soon*

ANIMAL EMERGENCY #3:
BAD LUCK LION

# DUCKS
# IN DANGER

### Emily Costello

### Illustrated by Larry Day

AN AVON CAMELOT BOOK

# For Laine, Elly and Jake Kolesar

This is a work of fiction. Names, characters, places and incidents either are the product of the author's imagination or are used fictitiously. If your pet is sick, please don't try to treat him yourself. Only qualified veterinarians can give the animals you love the care they need. Never approach wild animals. Being too close to humans may scare them. Also, they may bite or carry diseases.

AVON BOOKS, INC.
1350 Avenue of the Americas
New York, New York 10019

Copyright © 1999 by Emily Costello
Interior illustrations copyright © 1999 by Avon Books, Inc.
Interior illustrations by Larry Day
Published by arrangement with the author
Library of Congress Catalog Card Number: 98-93062
ISBN: 0-380-79754-2
www.avonbooks.com

First Avon Camelot Printing: March 1999

CAMELOT TRADEMARK REG. U.S. PAT. OFF. AND IN OTHER COUNTRIES, MARCA REGISTRADA, HECHO EN U.S.A.

Printed in the U.S.A.

OPM  10  9  8  7  6  5  4  3  2  1

# ACKNOWLEDGMENT

The author wishes to thank Tom Decker of the Vermont Fish and Wildlife Department for sharing his expertise on river otters.

● *1* ●

"**S**tella! Come quick!"

"Coming!" Nine-year-old Stella Sullivan dropped the book she was reading onto her Aunt Anya's desk. She ran down the hallway of the animal clinic.

Anya sounded upset, which set Stella's own heart racing. Usually Anya was completely calm. Especially when it came to treating the pets, livestock, and wild critters that were her patients in the clinic. Anya was the only veterinarian in Gateway, Montana. Stella wanted to be a vet when she grew up, so she spent as much time as possible hanging out with her aunt.

"In here!" Anya called.

Stella took a quick left into one of the treatment rooms.

A small boy was standing near the stainless-steel examining table. He looked like a rabbit. His front teeth were big and his white-blond hair was clipped so short that his ears stuck out. Stella could tell he'd been crying because he had a clean ribbon on each of his cheeks where tears had flowed. He was holding an oversized mayonnaise jar in his grimy hands.

Stella did a 180-degree turn. Anya and another woman were standing near the door, their backs against the wall. The woman's dark hair was smoothed back into a low ponytail. She had big ears, too—which made Stella guess she was the boy's mother.

"What's up?" Stella asked.

Anya cleared her throat and tried to look professional. "Thought you could help with this case. Kyle here has an injured tarantula. Quite an—impressive one, actually."

Stella knew a little bit about tarantulas. She'd done a book report about them for school—and gotten so interested that she'd wanted to get one for a pet. That hadn't happened because spiders freaked out Stella's mother, Norma. Well, Norma and Anya *were* identical twins. So maybe Anya was scared, too.

*I guess this is a case for me,* Stella thought. She was glad she had dropped by the clinic after school to raid Anya's collection of books about dog training.

Stella knelt down in front of the boy, so they were eye-to-eye. "What's your spider's name?"

"Charlotte." He sniffled, and wiped one cheek against his shoulder. "But she's sick."

"What happened to her?"

Fresh tears welled up in Kyle's brown eyes. "My little sister Margie ran over her with a Big Wheel."

"How about if I take a look?" Stella asked.

Wordlessly, Kyle held the jar out to her.

Stella took it. Standing up, she placed the jar on the examining table. The jar was empty except for a furry black spider about the size of Stella's hand. The tops of the spider's legs had brilliant yellowish orange patches.

"What a beauty," Stella said.

"She's a Mexican redknee," Kyle said proudly. "A *big* Mexican redknee."

Kyle stood up a little taller. "Almost four inches across," he said. "I've had her for two months already. My cousin raised her from a spiderling. Charlotte is the same age as me. Five."

Stella took a moment to think back on what she'd read about tarantulas. *They bite,* she reminded herself. The bites weren't any big deal— as long as you weren't allergic. Unfortunately, the only way to find out if you *were* allergic was to get bitten.

*No thanks,* Stella thought with a shudder. She remembered the book said you should never pick up a tarantula unless you knew it was calm. And how calm could Charlotte be feeling with a squished leg?

"Anya, where are the exam gloves?" Stella asked.

"In the drawer under the table," Anya said.

Stella opened the drawer, found the gloves, and pulled them on. The gloves were thin enough so that Stella's fingers didn't feel too clumsy. But she was pretty sure they would protect her from bites.

Another fact suddenly popped into Stella's mind. Tarantulas were fragile. Falling even a few feet could kill them. She moved the jar to the floor.

Kyle knelt down next to her.

Stella unscrewed the top of the jar. They waited a few moments, but Charlotte didn't budge. Stella lifted the jar's bottom about half an inch. The spider was now standing on a slight slope. She moved downhill and crawled out onto the floor. Now Stella could see that one of Charlotte's back legs was crushed. A clear, slightly bluish fluid was leaking out of the squashed leg and onto the dark fur that covered it. Tarantula blood.

"One of Charlotte's legs is hurt," Stella told Kyle.

Kyle took a deep quivery breath. "You can fix it, can't you?"

"Well . . ." Stella wanted to tell Kyle everything would be okay. But Charlotte's leg looked like a furry pancake. "I think I should cut the leg off."

"No!" Kyle dropped his head and started to sob.

"I'm not going to hurt Charlotte." Stella put a hand gently on Kyle's back. "Listen, it's not that bad. Charlotte is still going to have a bunch of legs left."

Kyle looked up. "Only seven."

"Seven's plenty," Stella said with a smile. "Now I want you to hold the jar in front of Charlotte so that she doesn't get away."

"Okay . . ." Kyle carefully positioned the jar and focused on his pet. "This is going to sting a little," he told her.

Stella glanced at her aunt.

Anya gave her a supportive smile. "Why don't you try pulling the leg off?" she suggested. "Most spiders can shed legs if they have to. Give the leg a firm yank, and I bet it will break off."

"Okay." Stella got up and opened one of the instrument drawers. She found a large tweezers and then knelt beside Charlotte and Kyle. Taking a deep breath, she grabbed the spider's injured leg. Charlotte crawled away, and the leg broke off near where it joined the body.

"It worked!" Stella reported.

Charlotte quickly turned around. Startled, Stella scooted back a little and dropped the tweezers. Charlotte crawled closer and picked at her injured leg.

"Oh, yuck!" Kyle said. "She's eating it."

Anya shrugged. "She's just trying to regain some of the nutrients she used growing it. Is she bleeding from the cut?"

Stella crawled around so that she could see. "No."

"Is that bad?" Kyle asked.

"No, it's good," Anya said. "I'm not a spider expert, but I know they lose lots of legs. Charlotte probably has a special muscle near her leg's base which allows her to close off the stump and stop the bleeding. Pretty handy, in my opinion."

Stella was still on her knees, examining the spider. "But Anya, she *is* still bleeding. From her—um, body, I think. There's a little dark spot by her tail and blood is coming out."

"You have to stop it," Anya said briskly.

Stella nodded. For the first time, she started to worry about Charlotte's life. Spiders could die from loss of blood just like people. "I think my book suggested plugging up holes with Super Glue," she said.

"I'll try to find some in the office." Anya hurried out into the hall. A moment later, she was back. "Nothing," she reported.

Kyle bit his lip. He looked down at Charlotte mournfully.

*Come on,* Stella told herself. *Think!* "Do we have anything else we could use?"

"Like what?" Anya asked.

"Um, that liquid stuff that works like a Band-Aid," Stella said. "Maybe rubber cement. Or some kind of paint if we could find a teeny brush."

"How about fingernail polish?" Kyle's mother asked.

"It's worth a try," Stella said.

"One problem," Anya said. "I haven't worn nail polish since—well, maybe never."

"I might have some." Kyle's mother pawed through her oversize purse. A moment later, she pulled out a tiny bottle and waved it over her head. "I found some!"

"Good work!" Stella grabbed the polish, gave it a quick shake, and unscrewed the top. A wee paintbrush was attached to the underside of the cap.

Stella gently dabbed the polish on the spider's wound.

Kyle looked uncertain. "Why are you doing Charlotte's nails?"

"This is to stop the bleeding," Stella explained. "But don't worry, the polish will fall off the next time Charlotte molts. Do you know what molting is?"

"Sure!" Kyle seemed eager to talk about his pet. "I can't wait to see it. Charlotte's gonna lose her whole skin—even the inside of her mouth."

Stella nodded. "Next time she molts, she'll have a tiny leg. And a few molts from now, she'll be as good as new."

"Cool!" Now Kyle looked almost excited.

Stella and Kyle gave the nail polish a few minutes to dry. Then Stella nudged Charlotte until she crawled into her jar.

"I want you to keep a close eye on Charlotte," Anya told Kyle from her spot near the door. "Bring her back if you see her bleeding."

"Okay," Kyle agreed.

"She'll be thirsty after losing all that blood," Stella put in. "So make sure she has plenty of moisture in her aquarium."

"And make sure the lid is on tight!" Kyle's mother added.

Kyle broke into a relieved smile as he picked up the jar and screwed on the lid. "I will," he promised.

"Come on," Kyle's mother said. "Let's get home and let your sister know that Charlotte is okay."

Kyle moved toward the door. He beamed up at Anya as he passed. "Thanks! Next time Charlotte molts, I'll bring her in so you can see her new leg."

Stella laughed at her aunt's horrified expression. "You'd better get used to Charlotte," she said. "Tarantulas live about twenty years. She could be your patient for a long time!"

## • 2 •

Stella opened her eyes and looked out the window of her bedroom. The sun was up. She rolled over in bed and glanced at her bedside clock—7:04.

*I'm late,* Stella thought with rising panic. *Four whole minutes late!*

Stella felt wide-awake now. She pushed back the covers and jumped up out of bed. She took the steps downstairs two at a time, careened through the living room, and skidded to a stop in front of the kitchen door.

Rufus, Stella's six-week-old puppy, was sitting in the middle of the kitchen floor. He was facing the doorway—as if he had been waiting for Stella to come down. The puppy was about the size of a cantaloupe. He had a pure white coat, and his bright black eyes sparkled merrily.

Stella's heart melted at the sight of his sweet, furry face. She loved dogs. But Rufus was special. Stella had adopted the puppy when he was only about two weeks old. He had been abandoned at a rest stop near Gateway.

The rest of his litter had died because they had been separated from their mother too soon. Rufus had almost died, too. Rose, an assistant sheriff in town, had found him just in time. She did what most people in Gateway did when they found an orphaned or abandoned animal: She called Anya.

Anya had announced that the puppy was too

young to live without round-the-clock nursing. So Stella had convinced her aunt to teach her how to feed the puppy with a stomach tube. She'd spent hours keeping the puppy warm by holding him against her skin. Rufus's survival had been touch-and-go for several days.

Now Rufus hardly seemed like the same dog. His old dish-towel limpness was gone. And his coat—which had been dull and dirty—gleamed.

Stella had worried that her family wouldn't like such a small dog. She'd stopped worrying when she saw how many presents her family bought the puppy.

Cora spent an entire week's allowance on a ball and a couple of squeeze toys. Jack had gotten Rufus a beautiful baby blue collar with tags. But Norma had topped them both. She'd ordered Rufus a special doggie kennel from some mail-order company back East.

"Hi, sweetie," Stella cooed. She stepped over the wooden toddler gate that kept Rufus in the kitchen. "Let's get you outside before it's too late."

Rufus ran in a little circle. Panting with excitement, he jumped up against Stella's calf.

Stella reached down to pet Rufus's head—and saw that she was too late. A wet spot stained the newspapers Stella had spread over the kitchen floor.

"Great," Stella muttered as she leaned over

and rolled up the soiled paper. She knew there was no point in scolding Rufus now. That only worked when you actually caught the dog in the act of peeing inside.

Carrying the soiled paper, Stella opened the door to the backyard. Rufus bounded out in front of her. While Stella tucked the newspaper into a garbage can, the puppy dashed around the fenced-in yard. He didn't stop to pee—which wasn't surprising since he had just gone.

Stella sat on the back steps and watched Rufus play. She loved him, but she was tired of cleaning up after him. Stella tried to take the puppy out first thing in the morning, last thing at night, and right after he ate. But her timing always seemed to be off.

Rufus dashed up to Stella. He was holding a plastic hamburger—his favorite squeeze toy—in his teeth.

Stella took the toy and tossed it across the yard. Rufus galloped after it like a tiny white horse, his pink tongue hanging. Stella wished she could ask her mom what she was doing wrong with Rufus's training.

Norma had been out of town for an entire week. Stella usually hated it when her mother traveled on business. But this time she was almost glad her mom had gone to Canada.

The back door opened, and Jack—Stella's father—came out onto the porch. "Morning, muffin."

"Hi, Daddy."

Stella's father was dressed for work in a pair of khaki pants and a dressy gray wool sweater. He was wearing his favorite wire-framed glasses. His salt-and-pepper hair still looked short and neat from its spring trim. Jack taught journalism at Montana State University.

Stella's father stood quietly sipping a cup of coffee. He looked out at the rocky, rugged mountains on the horizon. The sky was a soft blue. High overhead, fluffy white clouds raced by so quickly it looked as if someone had hit the fast-forward button.

Several acres of forest backed up onto the Sullivans' property. Even though it was only late April, the buds on the aspen trees were enlarging. As always, the air had a spicy pine twang.

Rufus had lost interest in his toy. Now he was circling the edge of the wooden fence, giving everything a good sniff.

Jack laid a hand on Stella's head. "Come on inside and have some cereal, muffin," he said. "You're going to have a big day today."

Stella leaned back and smiled up at her dad. "So's Mom," she said.

"Yup."

A jolt of excitement passed through Stella. She scrambled to her feet and clapped her hands for

Rufus to come. Jack and Stella went into the house together.

Stella's fourteen-year-old sister, Cora, was sitting at the wooden kitchen table. She'd already pulled out a box of cereal and a gallon of milk.

"Morning, Cora."

"Morning." Cora had dark hair and a wide mouth. She looked a lot like Jack.

Stella took after Norma and Anya. She had long red hair, which was curly enough to rat up if she didn't brush it every day. Her face was sprinkled with freckles. Her eyes were blue.

Cora leaned half out of her chair. "Hello, cutie pie," she called to Rufus.

Rufus responded by balancing on his hind legs and licking Cora's nose. Cora scooped him up and gave him a kiss in return.

"Not at the table," Jack said from his spot near the sink. He was rinsing out his coffee mug.

Cora put Rufus down.

"Come on, boy," Stella said. She took a bag of puppy chow out of a low cabinet and poured a tiny amount into Rufus's bowl. Since Rufus was such a small dog, he didn't eat much. Stella changed the puppy's water and laid some new newspaper on the floor.

Stella ate and got dressed quickly. Then she said good-bye to Rufus, Jack, and Cora and hopped on her bike for the quick ride to school.

John Colter Elementary was only about ten minutes' ride from the Sullivans'.

As she pedaled down the road into town, Stella took a deep breath of the chilly spring air. In another couple of months, school would be out for summer.

The road into town was much busier than usual. A steady stream of cars, RVs, and even TV news vans crawled by Stella.

Gateway was always full of tourists. The small town was just a few miles from an entrance to Goldenrock—the country's oldest and largest national park. Tourists swarmed there from all over the world. Most stopped in Gateway for a meal or a night's rest.

Stella pedaled across the school parking lot and locked her bike up in front of the low, flat-roofed building. She hurried down the corridor to Mrs. Jaffe's fourth grade classroom.

When Stella got into class, the room was buzzing. Nobody was sitting in their seats. Stella's teacher usually ran a tight ship. But today was unusual. The class was going on a field trip that morning. And not just *any* field trip. They were going to Goldenrock to witness the return of the gray wolf.

Stella felt like laughing, and singing, and dancing all at once. Her family had spent years working for the wolves' return. Now it was actually going to happen! She scanned the classroom, and spotted Josie standing near the window with Marisa Capra.

"Hi!" Stella greeted them.

"Hi." Josie was a petite girl. Her short black hair was so straight that it looked almost ironed. She had a doll's upturned nose and pretty almond-shaped blue eyes. She usually greeted the world with a smile, but today she seemed subdued.

"Guess what?" Marisa said. "Some TV reporters were in the parking lot when Josie and I got here. They interviewed us about the wolves!"

"You just missed them by about a minute," Josie said.

Stella didn't mind. She and Cora were cofounders of a group called Kids for Pups. Pups were what baby wolves were called. Over the winter, she and Cora had organized a big rally supporting the return of the wolves. They'd been on the evening news and in the local newspapers. Since then, reporters from all across the country had been calling them. Stella was glad her friends had gotten a chance to be interviewed for a change.

"What did you say?" Stella asked Marisa.

"I said it was a historical event," Marisa said.

"Cool!" Stella turned to Josie. "What did you say?"

"Nothing." Josie shifted her weight, looking down at her shoes.

"Oh."

Stella knew why Josie felt uncomfortable.

Josie was a ranch kid. Her father kept about a thousand head of cattle on a seven-hundred-acre ranch not far from Gateway. Mr. Russell was opposed to the reintroduction of wolves. And he was the kind of man who expected his children to share his beliefs. Josie's sixteen-year-old brother, Clem, had formed an antiwolf organization. He called it Kids for Common Sense. Josie seemed to have mixed feelings about the wolves. But she always defended her family's position. After all, she *was* a ranch kid.

Ranchers had feared and hated wolves for a long time. The ranchers and farmers who moved to Montana a hundred years ago had worried the wolves would gobble up their cattle and sheep—and their profits. So they'd shot and poisoned the wolves until they had disappeared from the entire western United States.

*But that was a long time ago,* Stella reminded herself. Scientists knew a lot more about wolves now. Like the fact that they hardly ever bothered livestock. And the fact that the rest of the animals in Goldenrock needed them.

The animals and plants in Goldenrock fit together like a huge motor. Each part, no matter how tiny, helped the motor run smoothly.

The wolves' job was keeping the populations of deer and elk from getting too big. Without the wolves, too many of those prey animals grazed on the parks' grasses and plants. That left nothing for other animals to eat. Meadow mice suffered. So did grizzly bears.

The only way to restore the motor to good running order was to bring the wolves back.

Stella considered reminding Josie about all this. But every time Stella and Josie tried to discuss the wolves, they ended up having a big argument. Now was definitely not a good time for a fight. So Stella decided to change the subject. "Rufus still isn't doing his business outside," she reported.

Marisa wrinkled her nose. "You have to wash the places where he goes with ammonia."

"Why?" Stella asked.

"To keep him from piddling in the same spot!" Josie laughed. "How come you didn't know that? You know everything about dogs."

Stella sighed. "Not about training them. But I'll try the ammonia. I'll try anything."

## • 3 •

On the bus later that morning, Stella choose a seat next to Josie. The girls sat quietly as the bus gasped and rolled down the familiar roads of Gateway.

A few miles outside of town, the kids piled out right next to the structure that had given the town its name—an enormous stone arch. The road into the park ran right under the span. When you crossed underneath, you entered Goldenrock.

"Line up, kids!" Mrs. Jaffe called.

Stella and Josie and their classmates took places along the road. Hundreds of people of all ages had gathered around the arch. And that was only the beginning of the crowd. As far as Stella could see, people were thronging the road inside the park. Cora's class was somewhere in the crowd.

And Jack and Anya had made plans to come to the park together. Stella hoped there wasn't an animal emergency that would keep her aunt away.

Television cameras were everywhere. Several dozen satellite vans lined the road. A throng of tourists had set up cameras and camcorders, too. Stella caught a few words of Spanish—and the babble of several other languages she didn't recognize.

"We have the perfect spot," Marisa said with excitement.

"I know!" Stella agreed.

Josie didn't say anything. Part of Stella felt sorry for her friend. She realized that as much as this day was a victory for her family, it was a defeat for Josie's.

Still, Stella had worked hard for this moment. And she couldn't let anyone—not even her best friend—ruin it for her.

*I want to remember this day,* Stella thought. She imagined herself as an old woman telling a group of children about the day the wolves returned to Goldenrock.

Suddenly, the crowd seemed to surge forward. Stella stood on her tiptoes. She caught sight of a green park-service car coming over the crest of the hill. Lights on the roof flashed blue and white. Another park-service car followed. And another.

People began to cheer as the line of vehicles made its way into the valley.

Behind the cars came a brown horse trailer. Stella's heart leapt at the sign of the trailer. She knew what was inside: eight specially constructed aluminum boxes that her mother had helped design.

Inside each box was a wolf.

The first of the park-service cars drew even with Stella and her friends. Stella caught a glimpse of her mother in the backseat of the second car.

"Hi, Mom!" Stella yelled—jumping up and down and waving.

Norma didn't see her. Her head was turned away from the car window and she was deep in conversation with another passenger. But Stella still felt good knowing her mother was back in town.

Stella's mom was a wildlife biologist at Goldenrock. She had been in Alberta, Canada, for the past week, helping trap the wolves and making sure they had a safe trip.

Canada wouldn't miss a few wolves. They had plenty—so many that it was legal to hunt them. The biologists had wanted to trap three complete wolf packs—or extended families. When Norma called a few days ago, she said they had only two.

Still, Norma said, the biologists were anxious to get the wolves they *had* captured back to the park. So the team split up. Some of the scientists stayed in Canada, where they'd try to capture more wolves. Another group packed up the eight wolves they'd already caught and headed for home.

This stretch of road was the last leg in the wolves' journey. Within an hour or so, they would be delivered to a special pen Norma and the other Goldenrock biologists had built for them.

The wolves would stay in the pen for several weeks, getting used to each other and their new surroundings. After this cooling-off period, the wolves would be set free in the park.

The pen was big—almost an entire acre. And it was far off in the woods. The pen was surrounded by ten-foot-high fences—plenty tall enough to keep the wolves in and the antiwolf people out.

Norma knew that many people—including maybe Josie's brother Clem—would consider it an honor to shoot the wolves before they could be released. So the Goldenrock staff had kept the pen's location a secret.

As the horse trailer zipped past, the crowd began to roar with excitement. A couple of people howled to show their approval.

Stella slipped Marisa an amused look.

Then she tilted her chin up, and let loose. *"Aaawh-hoooo, woof-woof-woof-aaawh-hoooo!"*

Marisa giggled, and then joined in. *"Aaawhooooo!"*

Stella had never heard a wolf howl in the wild. She had no idea if their howls sounded anything like real ones. But she hoped she would have a chance to find out soon.

# • 4 •

When Stella walked out of the school building that afternoon, she spotted her mother's truck idling at the curb. She ran over and yanked open the passenger door.

"Hi, Mommy!" Stella climbed half into the cab.

Norma leaned over and gave Stella a kiss on the cheek. "Hi, muffin. Let's hurry and get your bike in the flatbed. I want to get to the high school before your sister disappears."

Stella hesitated. She'd expected her mother to be bubbling with excitement about the wolves. But instead her face was drawn with worry. Her green parks department uniform looked slept in, and her hair needed combing.

*She's probably just tired,* Stella thought. She hurried over to the bike rack and quickly worked the combination on her lock. Stella was glad she didn't have to ride home. The wind was gusty, and the temperature had dropped since morning.

Stella wheeled the bike over to her mom's truck, and Norma helped her lift it into the flatbed. Soon Norma was turning out onto the main road.

Traffic was heavy. Norma inched the truck into a line of vehicles worming their way through town.

"Mom—is something wrong?"

Norma sighed, and nodded. She gave Stella a quick smile. "I'll explain once we pick up Cora. I don't want to go through the whole thing twice."

"Okay." Stella's excitement over seeing her mom was rapidly vanishing. An uneasy feeling had slithered into her stomach. She dreaded hearing her mother's news. Her mind churned with possibilities. Maybe Jack was sick. Or Anya.

Traffic was still crawling. Norma drove in silence for ten minutes before reaching the parking lot at the high school. She didn't ask any questions about Stella's week. She didn't tell any stories about Canada. Stella's worry deepened.

Cora was sitting on the high school's front steps, chatting with her best friend, May. When she saw Norma's truck, she jumped up and ran over.

"Hop in," Norma said.

Cora loaded her bike into the flatbed. Stella

scooted into the middle of the seat, and Cora sat next to the door. Norma rejoined the line of traffic.

"Mom—what's up?" Cora asked. "You're acting weird."

"I'm afraid I have some bad news," Norma said. "A group of ranchers and farmers has gotten a court order to stop the wolves' release."

Stella didn't understand. How could the release be stopped *now*? The wolves were already in the park.

"But I saw them this morning," Cora argued.

Norma nodded wearily. "The wolves are here, but we're not allowed to release them."

"The wolves aren't in their pen?" Stella was having a hard time absorbing this. She'd spent the afternoon imagining the wolves prowling their new home, sniffing the strange Goldenrock air.

"Actually they are in the pen," Norma reported. "But we're not allowed to let them out of their traveling cases."

Raindrops began pelting the windshield. Norma flicked on the wipers. Stella leaned forward so she could see the sky. A heavy, dark thunderhead towered above them. She wondered if the wolves were frightened by the sudden rain.

Norma sighed and shook her head. "Those cases are awfully small," she said, sounding distracted. "We designed them to keep the wolves calm during transport. Now they're stuck in the dark."

"Don't the cases have windows?" Cora asked.

"One little one," Norma said. "Good thing, too. The only way we can get them water is to squeeze ice cubes through the bars."

Stella imagined Rufus trapped in a tiny box. He wouldn't like that at all. "How do they pee?" she asked.

"They can't," Norma said. "Or maybe in the cage."

"How long do they have to stay locked up?" Cora asked.

"Until the court says they can be let out," Norma said with a disgusted shrug. "*If* the court says they can be let out."

"That's so unfair!" Now that the news was sinking in, Stella started to get mad.

"How long can they survive in the cases?" Cora asked.

"Maybe another twelve or twenty-four hours."

"That's it?" Stella asked.

"Well, remember, they've already had a long trip from Canada. And these are wild animals. Who knows how they feel being bumped around in airplanes and trucks. Smelling humans all the time. We always knew that the stress of transport could kill them. But now . . ."

The rain was coming down faster. Norma turned the wipers to high. *Whock. Whock. Whock.*

Even at the faster speed, they couldn't keep the windshield clean. Visibility was down to nothing. Norma slowed the truck.

Stella twisted around to face her mom. "Couldn't we send the wolves to a zoo? Then if the court decides they can be let go, we could get them back."

Norma smiled sadly. "That's a good idea, muffin. But wild wolves wouldn't survive in a zoo. We had a dozen wolf experts at headquarters today, and the only thing we could think to do was return the wolves to Canada. But I called the officials up there—and they said no way."

"So what happens if the court won't let you release them?" Cora asked.

Norma cleared her throat. "We'll have to put them down."

"Whoa." Cora shook her head and rubbed her fingers over her eyes.

"Isn't there some way we can make the court hurry?" Stella asked.

" 'Fraid not. This is a battle for the lawyers. All we can do is wait, and pray."

Suddenly, golf-ball-sized hailstones began to plink down on the road. Others hit the roof of the truck, making a hollow-sounding noise.

"Wow, this hail is huge." Cora sounded impressed.

"We'd better stop until this blows over." Norma pulled off to the side of the road and cut the engine. A red station wagon in front of her did the same.

Stella stared glumly out the window. She watched as the chunks of ice hit the ground with enough force to bounce back up again. Somehow the awful weather seemed to match her dark mood.

Cora and Norma were quiet, too—each apparently lost in her own gloomy thoughts.

Stella noticed that the red station wagon in front of them had Colorado plates. *Tourists,* she thought.

After a few minutes, the hail slowed. The din inside the cab dropped by about half. A moment later, the hail stopped altogether.

Norma started the truck again. "Let's hit the road. I need to get home and take a nap."

"When was the last time you slept?" Cora asked.

"Oh, about thirty hours ago." Norma pulled back onto the road, following the red station wagon. Now that they were outside town, traffic was much lighter. Norma turned into the small road that led to the Sullivans' house.

They were still following the station wagon, which wasn't too surprising. There were several small motels and campgrounds on the Sullivans' street.

A few miles from home, Stella saw an overweight squirrel on the side of the road. Her plush

upright tail twitched nervously. The squirrel hesitated until the red car was almost even with her.
Then it ran into the street. The red car
swerved right.

Norma hit the brakes.

The squirrel cleared the road in a few hops and
disappeared into the woods on the far side.

Stella heard a sickening metallic crunch. That
was mixed with the sound of glass shattering—
and people screaming. The red car had gone off
the road and hit a tree!

"My God," Norma breathed.

The car was teetering on its two right wheels.

Stella's eyes widened in horror as it slowly tipped to the right, and rolled over onto its roof. The car slid a few yards down the embankment and stopped.

## • 5 •

**N**orma pulled onto the shoulder, braked, and slammed the truck into PARK. She and Cora threw open their doors and jumped out. Stella started to wiggle across the seat, moving to follow them.

"Stella—I want you to stay here," Norma said. "Call 911 on the portable phone."

"But Mom—"

Norma didn't stop to listen. She jogged off toward the overturned car.

Stella fiddled with the knob on the glove compartment, where her mom kept the portable phone. Her hands were shaking as she flipped open the phone and pushed 9-1-1. She kept hearing that metallic crunch in her mind, and it made her queasy.

"Good afternoon, Goldenrock Police and Fire," came a calm voice. "This is Operator 3. Do you have an emergency?"

"Yes," Stella said. "A car just hit a tree and flipped over." Saying those words made Stella feel weepy, and she took a deep breath to steady herself.

"Where are you?" the operator asked.

"In my mom's truck," Stella explained. Then she realized that wasn't what the operator needed to know. "Oh—we're on Rural Route 2A, just down from where it crosses 98. But the car that crashed isn't on the road anymore. It slid off."

"Okay, police officers are on their way," the operator said. "I've requested an ambulance. Let me ask you a few more questions. Is the car on fire?"

Stella peered through the window. The sun had come out from behind the massive dark clouds, which made it difficult to see if any flames were around the car. "I don't think so."

"Can you tell if anyone is hurt?"

"My mom and sister went to check," Stella said. "We heard screaming during the crash. Wait—it looks like my mom is helping some people crawl out!"

"Do they look okay?"

"I don't know. My mom is in the way. I can't see."

"Can you talk to her?" the operator asked.

"Sure!" Stella was dying to find out what was going on. The operator seemed to be giving her permission to do just that.

"I have to get out of the truck," Stella explained. "Hold on."

"I'll stay on the line until the officers get there," the operator promised.

Still holding the phone, Stella crawled over to the passenger's side and hopped down. She could hear a siren howling in the distance.

Norma and Cora were standing on the side of the road next to a man and a boy about Cora's age. They were looking down at the overturned car and talking in low voices.

The man was wearing dark corduroys and an ugly green-and-blue-plaid golf jacket. He was going bald on top. The boy was handsome, with messy blond hair. His head snapped in Stella's direction as she approached—as if he was startled by the sound of her footsteps. But he didn't meet Stella's eyes.

"Mom? The 911 operator wants to know if anyone is hurt."

"We're fine," the man said. "A few scratches is all."

"Stella, stay away from the car," Norma said sharply. "It could explode."

"Dad?" The boy sounded alarmed.

The man jerked to attention. "Explode? What makes you say that?"

"Well, the gas tank . . ." Norma said.

"Queenie is still in there!" The boy sounded like he was about to cry.

"Don't worry, Devon, I'll get her." The man started down the embankment toward the car, slipping on the hail-spotted underbrush.

"Wait!" Norma yelled. "Wait for the ambulance. Please!"

The man didn't pay any attention. He scrambled the last few feet to the car and began tugging on the upside-down rear door.

Stella put the phone to her ear. "Are you still there?"

"Yes," the operator said. "The officers are almost there. What's happening?"

"Someone is still in the car." As soon as the words were out, Stella realized she'd made a mistake. The man had gotten the door open. He was pulling a *dog* out of the car.

"Oh no," Cora said.

"What's wrong?" the boy—Devon—demanded.

Stella looked at the dog, her heart starting to rat-a-tat in her chest. Queenie was a full-grown chocolate Labrador retriever. Her head and side were covered with blood. She was limp—either unconscious or dead.

Norma took a few steps down the embankment. "Give her to me! I can help."

The man put Queenie in Norma's arms, and

scrambled the rest of the way up the embankment.

Norma gently laid Queenie down in the grass on the side of the road.

"Cora, can you talk to 911?" Stella held out the phone.

"Sure." Cora took the phone.

Stella rushed over to her mom and Queenie.

Norma glanced up at her. "I can't get a heartbeat. Will you help me do CPR?"

Stella nodded. She had watched Anya do CPR on dogs several times. And after she had brought Rufus home, Norma had given her a lesson. Stella wanted to be prepared in case Rufus ever got hurt.

"I'll do the breathing," Stella offered.

Norma nodded, and moved into position on Queenie's side. "Make sure nothing's in her mouth," she said.

Stella gently opened Queenie's mouth. She didn't see any strange objects, but Queenie's limp tongue had slipped back. Stella grabbed the tip of the tongue with her fingers and pulled it forward. Then she gently pushed the dog's jaws together.

She did her best to seal Queenie's lips with her hand, but her hand was too small to reach all the way around the dog's mouth. Well, it would have to do.

"I'm ready," Stella told her mom.

"Go ahead and start."

Stella took a deep breath and placed her lips over Queenie's gumdrop-shaped nose. The dog's whiskers tickled her cheeks. Stella blew in steadily, counting *one, two, three* to herself. Out of one eye, she could see Queenie's chest expand slightly.

*Thirty seconds before the next breath,* Stella reminded herself. She sat back and watched her mother work.

Queenie was wearing an elaborate harness-style leash which fastened around her chest. Norma fumbled with the buckles, loosening it as quickly as she could.

Stella glanced up and saw Devon—still standing in the same spot. She tried to give him a reassuring smile, but the boy didn't respond.

Norma had gotten the harness off. She placed the heel of her hand on Queenie's chest and pushed down firmly. Stella watched closely as Norma released the pressure, then immediately pushed down again. Norma kept pushing and releasing until she had compressed Queenie's chest six times. Then she laid her hand on the dog's chest, feeling for a heartbeat. With a slight shake of her head, she began a new series of compressions.

Stella leaned over and breathed again into the dog's nose. *One, two, three.* She felt her anxiety rising. She wasn't sure how long they had to get Queenie's heart beating again. Four minutes at the most, she guessed. After that, the lack of

blood flow would cause blindness or brain damage.

She wondered how long ago the dog had stopped breathing. Surely more than four minutes had passed since the car had gone off the road.

When Norma finished another set of compressions, she laid her hand on Queenie's chest again. But this time she smiled. "Bingo! I feel a faint heartbeat. Let me see if she's breathing."

Stella scooted out of the way. She watched as her mother leaned her cheek up almost against Queenie's nose.

"She's breathing!" Norma reported.

"That's great." Stella let out a relieved sigh. She heard a car slow down to see what was happening, then speed up again.

"We're not out of the woods yet," Norma said. "Queenie's lost a lot of blood. We've got to control the bleeding and get her to the clinic fast."

Stella forced her attention back to the dog. Now wasn't the time to relax. They still had work to do.

Norma examined Queenie. The dog's brow and broad chest were covered with a series of small cuts. Stella thought it looked as if she had been thrown against the shattered windshield. Something—perhaps a piece of glass—had sliced the dog's left ear so that a flap of fur-covered skin hung loose.

"The bleeding around the head has stopped," Norma reported. "Now, let's see how that leg looks."

Norma made *tsk, tsk* noises as she looked at Queenie's leg.

Stella forced herself to take a peek. What she saw made her cover her mouth with one hand. A baseball-sized hunk of flesh had been gouged out of Queenie's upper thigh. The fur around the ugly wound looked sticky and slick with blood.

Without thinking about it, Stella moved back a few feet.

"Are you okay?" Norma asked.

"Um, fine." The truth was, Stella felt dizzy. But she didn't want to admit that to her mom. She didn't want anything to distract Norma from taking care of Queenie.

Norma didn't seem to notice Stella's hesitation. "Good," she muttered. "Now we need something to use as a dressing."

"Like what?"

"A clean cloth . . ."

Stella immediately pulled her sweatshirt over her head. "Use this."

Norma grabbed the sweatshirt and folded it in fourths. She pressed it into Queenie's wound. "Can you hold this?" she asked Stella.

Stella felt her stomach do a slow roll, but she nodded. She moved closer to Queenie and held the sweatshirt in place with the flat of her hand.

"Okay," Norma said. "Keep pressure on the wound and watch to make sure she doesn't stop breathing. I'll be right back."

Stella sat quietly, watching Queenie's chest rise and fall. She wondered if Queenie was in pain, and whether she'd live. Stella felt sorry for Queenie's owners, especially Devon. She knew how unhappy she'd be if Rufus was in an accident.

Part of Stella was aware of the scene unfolding around her. Norma was having an intense conversation with Devon and his dad. A cruiser from the sheriff's department had pulled up. And Cora was doing something in the back of Norma's truck—maybe getting the bikes out.

Norma came jogging back. "Okay, let's load her into the truck."

Stella moved out of the way as her mother stooped down and picked up the dog, doing her best to keep the sweatshirt in place. Queenie's elaborate harness fell onto the ground. Stella retrieved it, planning to give it back to Devon. She trotted alongside as Norma moved quickly to the back of the truck.

Cora had unfolded an old red-and-black wool blanket Norma kept in the truck. Norma laid the dog on top. The blanket would give Queenie a little padding against the hard flatbed bottom.

"I'll ride in the back, too," Stella offered. "That

way I can keep the pressure on Queenie's wound."

Norma considered for a second—probably wondering if riding in the bed was safe. "I guess that's okay."

She turned to Cora. "We'll see you at home in a little while."

"Good luck," Cora said.

Devon and his father approached. "The sheriff offered to bring us by the clinic as soon as we take care of the car and the paperwork," Devon's dad said.

"Please take good care of her," Devon added.

"We'll do our best," Norma said. She slammed the flatbed gate shut. "Let's go!"

## • 6 •

Stella sat cross-legged on the bed of the truck. She gently put pressure on Queenie's wound. Blood was beginning to soak through the material. Queenie's body was limp, her eyes closed, her tongue hanging slack.

Norma started up the truck, did a three-point turn, and headed into town. As soon as they were on the road, she reached back and opened the window that divided the cab from the bed. "Everything okay?" she asked.

"Queenie is starting to shake. Like she's cold or something." Stella watched as the dog's muscles trembled.

"See if you can find anything back there to cover her up."

Stella felt around with her free hand and came

up with an old raincoat of her father's. She pulled it over Queenie's middle—leaving her head and hind legs free.

Norma picked up the portable phone, called Anya, and warned her they were on their way.

When they pulled up to the clinic a few minutes later, Anya was waiting outside. The moment Norma stopped the truck, she pulled open the gate to the flatbed and leaned in to get a look at the dog. Queenie was still twitching and shaking.

Stella watched as her aunt lifted Queenie's upper lip. She knew Anya was examining Queenie's gums. Pale gums were a sign of internal injury, among other things.

"How do they look?" Stella asked.

"Pale. This puppy is in shock. Let's get her inside."

Shock? Stella didn't know what that meant, but it didn't sound good.

Anya grabbed two corners of the blanket. "Get the other end," she told Stella.

Stella picked up the corners on her side, lifted them as high as she could, and duck-walked toward the end of the truck. Queenie let out a moan.

Norma was waiting on the sidewalk. She took the blanket out of Stella's hands and helped Anya carry Queenie up the walkway to the clinic.

As Stella hopped out of the flatbed, her foot

caught on something. She looked back. Queenie's leash was looped around her sneaker. Stella pulled it loose and carried it with her.

A few minutes later, Queenie was lying on the stainless-steel table in one of Anya's examining rooms. Anya was scrubbing her hands at the sink.

"What's shock?" Stella asked.

Norma gave Stella a weary smile. "Basically, it's poor blood flow. Queenie's heart is only working about half-time."

Anya came back to the table and began to work, her movements sure and efficient. She gave Queenie a shot of medicine to put her to sleep. While the medicine began to take effect, she shaved a small patch of fur off one of Queenie's uninjured front legs. She inserted a needle into a vein and attached a bag of canine blood. She also inserted a catheter—a slender tube that would draw Queenie's pee into a bag.

Then Anya removed Stella's now-soggy sweatshirt from the wound and clipped the fur from around it. She used a damp wad of gauze to gently clean the wound's edges.

"Could someone get me a tweezers and some water?" Anya asked without taking her eyes off her work. "Oh—and a bulb syringe."

"Where do you—" Norma started.

"Don't worry, Mom. I'll get them." Stella quickly put the leash down on a chair. She moved to the glass-fronted cabinets near the sink, got what her aunt needed, and hurried back to the table.

"Thanks." Anya drew water into the syringe—which looked like a turkey baster. She squeezed the water into Queenie's wound.

"Looks like she picked up some glass." Anya used the tweezers to pick up a blood-smeared chunk of safety glass. She held it up to the strong overhead light.

"Poor girl," Norma said.

A tense ten minutes passed as Anya carefully inspected every inch of Queenie's wound and pulled out a small handful of glass. Finally, she sighed. "I think I've got it all. Let's close this nasty thing up. Stella, could you find me some thread and a needle?"

Stella smiled a little as she realized that Anya was about to sew up Queenie's wound. The worst was over. She delivered the materials to her aunt, then ran her fingers over the smooth fur on Queenie's cheek.

"You're going to be okay now, girl," Stella murmured.

Anya glanced up. "Well, I'm not so sure about that. Queenie here has had a difficult afternoon. She's still in pretty dicey condition."

"Are you going to do some X-rays?" Norma asked.

"Maybe . . ."

Stella heard a faint knock coming from the front of the building. "Someone's here."

"I'll get it," Norma offered.

Stella went to sit down, and noticed Queenie's harness. She picked it up. "Have you ever seen a leash like this before?" she asked her aunt.

Anya gave a quick glance. "Sure. It's a harness for a companion dog."

"What's a companion dog?"

"You know, a dog that helps a blind or deaf person get around," Anya explained.

Devon definitely wasn't deaf, Stella thought as she looked down at the harness. But maybe he was blind. That would explain why he hadn't met her gaze earlier.

Stella glanced up at Queenie. The big brown dog was still knocked out from the anesthetic and loss of blood. Her breathing was shallow.

*Don't die,* Stella prayed. Queenie was no ordinary dog. She could guess how much Devon needed her.

Stella heard her mother's voice and turned toward the door. Norma came back into the room—followed by Devon and his father. Devon was holding a white cane.

Anya stepped forward. "Hi, I'm Norma's sister, Anya."

Devon's father held out his hand. "David Martins."

The adults began talking about the accident— where the Martins's car had been towed, where they could find a motel room, and what Anya had done for Queenie.

Stella glanced over at Devon. She could see now that his eyes didn't look quite normal. They were a pretty brown color, but looked somehow blank—like a window with the shades drawn.

Devon seemed unsure of himself, but he was slowly inching away from his father's side. His left hand was outstretched, right hand tapping the cane. Stella had a good idea what he was looking for.

She cautiously approached the boy's side. "Hi. I'm Stella. Do you want to—um, see Queenie?"

Devon immediately broke into a relieved grin. "Could I?"

"Sure. She's right over here. She hasn't woken up yet. Here, take my hand."

Stella reached out and grasped Devon's hand. She gently led him across the room to the table. Devon tested the table side with his free hand. Then he gently patted the tabletop until he found Queenie's head.

A strangled sound escaped from Devon's throat. He put his head down on the tabletop. "Oh, Queenie," he cried. "Please get better."

Stella felt her own eyes fill with tears. She looked at the adults, who were still standing near the door.

Her mother's face was creased with worry.

Anya shook her head sadly.

Mr. Martins came forward, and put a hand on Devon's back. "I'm sure the vet has done everything possible."

"My aunt is a really good vet," Stella put in.

Devon lifted his head and tried to blink back his tears.

Mr. Martins took his elbow and led him toward the door. "I'm sorry for the upset," he told Anya in a low voice. "It's just that Devon waited a long time to get old enough to have a companion dog. He's spent the past month in Seattle getting to know Queenie—and getting used to having his independence back. And now, on the way home . . ."

"She's got to get better." Devon's tone was completely hopeless.

"I promise to do my best," Anya said stoutly.

"Come on, Dev. Let's get out of the way and let the vet work." Mr. Martins gave them all a solemn nod. "Sheriff Rose is waiting outside. She's going to take us to the motel. We'll come back tomorrow morning to check on Queenie."

"Sounds fine," Anya agreed.

Norma and Stella walked out onto the clinic steps. They watched as the Martins climbed into the patrol car.

"Poor kid," Norma said with a sigh.

## • 7 •

The ride home was uneventful. Stella and Norma walked in the back door just in time to see Cora wadding up a roll of newspaper. The smell of doggy poop was strong. Rufus was sniffing around at the exposed tiles.

Stella groaned. "Mom, Rufus is *still* going inside."

Norma dumped her purse on the kitchen table. "Oh, I'm not surprised. These things take time. It took me *months* to potty train you two."

Cora and Stella exchanged horrified looks. Stella definitely didn't want to hear any more about *that*. She opened the back door. "Thanks for cleaning up, Cora. Come on, Ruf! Let's go out!"

Rufus bounded through the open door. He almost tripped on the back steps in his rush to get to the yard.

Watching the puppy made Stella giggle. She found his hamburger chew toy at the bottom of the steps, and tossed it across the yard. "Go get it, boy!"

Rufus galloped off, his tiny legs a blur of speed.

Stella and Rufus played catch for another ten minutes. Rufus showed no sign of slowing down, but Stella was starting to get chilly without her sweatshirt. She'd just decided to go inside when Cora came out to the back porch.

"Phone for you."

"Coming." Stella dashed up the stairs with Rufus on her heels. She took the phone from Cora and went into the kitchen. Rufus went straight to his bowl and began lapping up water. Cora sat back down at the table, where she was reading her science textbook.

"Hello?"

"Stella. It's Josie."

Josie's voice sounded wrong. Too no-nonsense.

"What's the matter?" Stella asked.

"I'm taking care of Clem's ducks." Josie's explanation came out in a rush. "He's off elk hunting with some friends. You know how Clem loves those ducks."

Stella nodded even though Josie couldn't see her. Josie had told her all about her brother's ducks. Clem thought the Russells could make a lot of money selling them. He'd convinced his dad to let him run the little enterprise. Clem had selected a breed and ordered fifteen ducklings from Wyoming. He'd spent hours of his free time building a luxurious duck coop.

"You said he's planning to raise enough money for a new horse with 'em," Stella said.

"Right . . . But, Stella, I did something really stupid. I left the door to the duck coop open!"

Stella knew it wasn't a big deal if the ducks got out. Since they ate in the coop, they always returned there at night. That only left one possibility. "Did something get in?"

"A fox."

Stella cringed.

The red foxes which lived in that part of Montana were skilled hunters. During winter, they kept their bellies full by diving snout first into deep snow and snatching up little rodent-appetizers called voles. Catching Clem's ducks must have seemed almost too easy.

The ducks were American Pekings. They were raised in coops, like chickens. The breed had long since lost its ability to fly—which meant they wouldn't have any way of protecting themselves from a fox.

"I heard the ducks squawking like mad and found the fox out there," Josie was saying. "I chased him, and he ran off with a duckling still hanging from his mouth. I found another one dead. And a third injured."

"Sounds like you did a good job," Stella said. "Another few minutes and the fox might have killed them all."

Josie made an exasperated groan. "Clem won't look at it that way. Anyway, I'll worry about him later. Right now, we've got to help the injured duck."

Stella thought for a minute. "Where's Mom?" she asked Cora.

"Sleeping."

Norma would probably nap for a few hours, which meant dinner would be late. Stella wasn't sure where her dad was, but he wasn't home yet. Nobody would mind if she went back into town.

"Did you call Anya?"

"I caught her on her portable phone. She's out on a call, dehorning cattle at some ranch up by Fourteenmile River. She said we should do what we can on our own."

*Poor Anya,* Stella thought. Fourteenmile River wasn't that far from Gateway, but a mountain range lay between the two small towns. Anya would have to head north, then south on the other side of the peaks. She had a long drive ahead of her.

And dehorning cattle was a sweaty, difficult job. Chances were Anya wouldn't be back until after midnight. Stella guessed Queenie's emergency had probably delayed her aunt's departure for the ranch.

"Can you meet me at the clinic?" Stella asked Josie.

"That's what I've been asking you!" Josie hollered.

"Okay, see you in fifteen minutes," Stella said. "Wait—how are you going to get the duck into town?"

"I found an old picnic basket in the barn. See you." Josie hung up.

Stella quickly scribbled a note to her folks, explaining where she was going. Then she went outside, got her bike out of the back of the truck, and pedaled into town. She got to the clinic before Josie, so she unlocked the door with her key.

When she turned on the lights, Anya's big basset hound, Boris, came out of the office to see what was going on. He moved lazily, his toenails clicking on the linoleum floor. Stella paused long enough to run one of Boris's long soft ears through her fingers and smooth back the wrinkles on his forehead. Boris let his hind leg slide sideways, flopping down on his rear. He seemed content to sit in the hallway for the rest of his life.

But when Stella clapped her hands and pointed to Anya's office, Boris hauled himself to his feet and trotted off. Anya had trained Boris to stay in the office while the clinic was open. He had a comfortable snoozing bed under her desk.

Stella went back to the boarder room to check on Queenie. The boarder room was where Anya kept animals that had to stay over at the clinic. Stella and Josie had helped nurse dozens of boarders back to health. If the boarders were wild, the girls often went with Anya to release them in the woods.

Anya had settled Queenie in the quietest and most comfortable kennel. The big dog was sleeping on her side, her wounded leg on top. Stella drew close enough to see the comforting rise and fall of Queenie's chest. She poked a few fingers through the wire and stroked one chocolate paw.

*Queenie is beautiful,* Stella thought. She wondered how much more beautiful the dog was when she was healthy. She could imagine Queenie confidently moving down the sidewalk with Devon at her side.

Stella closed her eyes and imagined being blind. She pretended she would never see Rufus's furry little face again. Or her mom's or dad's or Cora's.

She imagined never being able to see stars, or daffodils, or a salmon flashing in a stream. Could blind people be veterinarians? Probably not. Stella shuddered and opened her eyes.

Queenie lay motionless in front of her. Being blind would be awful. But maybe it would be a little less awful with the help of a dog like Queenie.

"Stella! We're here! Where are you?"

"Coming!" Stella rushed to the front of the clinic.

Josie was standing in the hallway outside Anya's office. She was carrying a dark wooden picnic basket. "She's been quacking the whole ride here," Josie complained.

Stella smiled. "That's probably a good sign. She must not be hurt bad. Let's see her." She led Josie into an examination room.

Josie cautiously opened one of the basket's flaps and lifted the duck out. She held on to her as Stella did a quick examination.

The duck was a typical American Peking. She looked plain and plump compared to a colorful and muscular wild duck. Her body was shaped like a brick with rounded edges. She'd lost her yellow baby feathers. At about ten weeks old—almost full-grown—her feathers were pure white. Her bright orange feet and black eyes stood out in great contrast.

Stella had to admit that the duck looked the picture of health. Her breast muscles were well developed, which was a sign she had been eating well. Plus, she had a healthy wariness of Stella.

"Does she have a name?" Stella asked.

Josie gave her a get-real look. "Can you imagine Clem naming his ducks?"

"Not really. Well, let's call her Stumpy."

She chose that name because one of the duck's feet was injured. The webbed part looked fine. But higher up—near where the leg joined the abdomen—Stella saw an ugly red gash. Apparently the fox had taken a quick chomp on Stumpy's leg. A small rust-colored spot stained the duck's snowy breast.

"This doesn't look so bad," Stella reported. "We'll just have to clean and bandage these bites."

Josie's entire manner relaxed. "Do you really think she'll live?"

"I don't see why not," Stella said.

"Oh—Anya told me we shouldn't use any stitches on the bites because they'd probably get infected."

"Okay. Hold her steady. Let's start with the breast."

Stella had a difficult time seeing the injury. The feathers grew densely on the duck's chest.

Gently, Stella blew. She'd seen Anya do that to part eagle feathers. The feathers moved long enough for her to spot an angry-looking gash. But the second she stopped blowing, the feathers fell back together again.

Stumpy did not seem to enjoy this examination. She held her head sideways so that she could keep one tiny black eye on Stella. The duck's angry gaze made Stella uncomfortable, and she took a step back.

"I'm not sure how we can clean that bite," Stella told Josie. "The feathers are in the way."

"What would Anya do?"

"Well, with a dog or a cat she would trim the fur around the wound."

"So pluck some feathers. And hurry up. Stumpy doesn't really like hanging out on my lap."

Stumpy *was* wiggling to get free. She kept extending her neck and attempting to loosen Josie's grip.

Stella knew she had to work fast—but still she hesitated. "Pluck her feathers?" she asked. "Won't that hurt?"

Josie shrugged. "Probably a little. But the ducks do it all the time. For some reason, they like to eat them."

"Okay, just a second." Stella had made a decision. She quickly crossed the room and opened one of Anya's glass-fronted cabinets. She pawed through the contents until she found what she wanted—a spray can of local anesthetic.

She hurried back to the exam table. Blowing on Stumpy's feathers to expose the wound, she sprayed several quick blasts onto the duck's chest.

Stumpy reared her head back in surprise. But as soon as the spraying stopped, she relaxed.

Stella knew that the spray would make the duck's skin a little numb. She hoped that would lessen the pain of having her feathers plucked.

Again, Stella blew. When she could see the wound, she grasped a bordering feather and pulled. The feather resisted slightly, then came free.

The feathers on Stumpy's chest were small. Stella gently plucked for almost ten minutes until she had cleared an area around the wound.

While she worked, Stella tried to decide whether she should ask Josie about the wolves. She wondered if Mr. Russell was one of the ranchers who had talked the judge into keeping the wolves locked up in their traveling pens.

"Hey! Don't pluck so many," Josie said, interrupting Stella's thoughts. "Clem will freak if he comes home to a bald duck."

"Right," Stella said, forcing herself to concentrate on what she was doing. She had a clear view of Stumpy's wound now. "The bite doesn't look too bad."

"Good," Josie said. "My arms are getting tired."

Stella quickly cleaned out the chest wound with a little hydrogen peroxide. Then she dabbed on some antibiotic ointment and taped some gauze over the wound.

"Now for the leg," Stella said.

Josie groaned. "Please hurry."

Stella was glad the leg wound was easier to work on. She was able to clean and bandage it quickly.

Josie heaved an enormous sigh as she placed Stumpy back in the picnic basket. "Thanks, Stella. You saved my life."

Stella made a face. "No biggie. But you're going to have to change those bandages once a day until Stumpy's wounds heal."

"I will," Josie promised. "Listen, I'd better get Stumpy home."

"What are you up to this weekend?" Stella asked as the girls turned off the lights and headed toward the front of the clinic.

Josie sighed. "I have a pile of chores to do. Without Clem around, we're a little overwhelmed."

As the girls walked outside together, Stella decided not to mention the wolves. Even if Mr. Russell was involved, Josie wouldn't be able to change his mind.

Josie put the picnic basket down as she and Stella collected their bikes.

"I'll see you Monday," Josie said.

"Bye!" Stella got on her own bike and headed home. She wasn't sure what time it was, but the sun had already disappeared behind the mountains. Directly overhead the sky was dark. But it lightened in degrees toward the horizon, turning first a deep purple, then lavender, then cantaloupe orange.

Stella began to pedal faster. She was anxious to get home for dinner. And besides, she was shivering. Without the sunshine, the temperature had dipped even further.

At home, Stella found Cora and Jack busy in the kitchen. Cora was shaking Tabasco sauce into an enormous pot of chili. A delicious spicy smell filled the room.

Jack gave Stella a kiss. "Why did you go back to the clinic?"

"To patch up one of Clem Russell's ducks," Stella said. She gave Rufus a quick pat hello and went to the sink to wash her hands.

Cora turned away from the stove and stared openmouthed at Stella. "You did something to help *Clem*?"

Stella felt a quick stab of guilt. As far as Cora was concerned, Clem Russell's name was dirt. Truth was, Stella wasn't too fond of him either.

Clem had done everything possible to keep wolves out of Goldenrock. He'd even tried to ruin the Kids for Pups rally Cora and Stella had organized. It was people like Clem who were keeping the wolves locked up. But that didn't mean she could refuse to help Stumpy.

Stella gave Cora an apologetic smile. "I didn't do it to help Clem," she explained. "I did it for the duck."

## • 8 •

**D**inner at the Sullivans' that evening was subdued. Norma crawled out of bed long enough to
eat, but she was half-asleep and not very talkative.

Everyone was worried about the wolves. Mack,
one of Norma's coworkers, called to say that the
lawyers were still fighting it out.

At least the chili was good. Stella devoured two
big helpings over brown rice. She was full to the
groaning point.

Stella helped Jack with the dishes, then took
Rufus outside. The puppy romped around in the
grass—but refused to do any business. *He's probably saving it up until he goes inside,* Stella
thought. She shut Rufus in the kitchen and
crawled into bed with a book called *The Art of
Raising a Puppy*. She was on page two.

The book was still propped up on Stella's chest when she was startled awake sometime during the night. She heard someone pick the phone up in the middle of a ring.

It was late. The backyard and the woods beyond were hidden by deep darkness. No cars were passing on the road that ran in front of the house.

Stella's clock said 2:36. That was too late for phone calls—unless someone was calling with news about the wolves!

Suddenly feeling much more awake, Stella climbed out of bed and slipped into the hallway. She could hear the murmur of her mother's voice coming from her parents' bedroom. Their door was open a crack, so Stella pushed it open.

"Mom?"

Norma was lying in bed. She was just hanging up the phone as Stella tiptoed in. Norma put her finger to her lips and nodded sideways toward Jack. He was lying on his back, his eyes covered with his arm. Norma slipped out of bed.

"Was that about the wolves?" Stella whispered.

"Yes." Even though Norma was speaking very low, Stella could hear the excitement in her voice. "A higher court overruled the order stopping the wolves' release."

"We can let them out?"

"Yup!"

Stella watched as her mother crossed to the

closet. She pulled out her jeans, a flannel shirt, and a pair of waterproof boots.

"Are you going now?" Stella asked.

"Absolutely." Norma stepped into the jeans. "I want the wolves released immediately. Mack is going to meet me at the pen."

Stella suddenly felt wide-awake. "Can I come? Please?"

Norma considered as she pulled on her shirt. "Muffin, it's the middle of the night. . . ."

"I won't be able to sleep anyway," Stella argued. "Please?"

Norma nodded slowly. "Okay then. Meet me downstairs in two seconds."

"Thanks, Mom!" Stella rushed back to her room and quickly put on some warm clothes and hiking boots. She was waiting in the kitchen when her mom came down.

Rufus was sacked out in his kennel—curled up with his head resting on his front paws. His newspapers were still dry. For now.

Norma quietly opened the kitchen door, and they stole down the back steps. Stella shivered— partly from the night chill and partly from happiness. They climbed into the car, and Norma fired it up. She pulled out onto 2A, which was deserted, then flipped on the heater.

Thousands of stars brightened the night sky. As they turned onto the main highway, Stella could see that the moon had just risen over the distant mountains. It seemed to hover above the road like an enormous hot-air balloon. The moonlight reflected off the snow-covered peaks.

"The moon is almost full," Stella said.

Norma gave her a brief smile. "Good night to let a few wolves free."

Stella giggled.

The pair grew quiet as Norma drove the moonlit roads into the park. Before long, she pulled onto the side of the road behind Mack's green park-service jeep. Norma retrieved a couple of flashlights from the glove compartment. They climbed out.

"Ready for a walk?" Norma asked.

"You bet!" Stella tried to sound wide-awake, so her mother wouldn't change her mind and make her stay in the car.

"Remember, muffin, the location of the pen is top secret—"

"What do you think I'm going to do?" Stella asked. "Publish the coordinates on the Internet?"

Norma gave her a don't-get-smart-with-me look.

"Seriously, Mom. I want the wolves safe as much as you do."

"Okay. Let's go." Norma led the way into the aspen and lodgepole pine woods. She followed an unmarked path that Stella could barely make out.

Stella turned on her flashlight and trotted after

her mother. She didn't want Norma to get too far ahead. The woods at night were creepy. Stella could hear a distant tree creaking as it twisted in the breeze. Every so often leaves crunched as some animal—maybe a deer—heard them coming and darted off through the forest.

But Stella didn't have much time to observe her surroundings. Norma set a blistering pace. Before long Stella grew uncomfortably hot in her sweatshirt. She pulled it over her head and tied it around her waist.

Just when Stella was getting ready to ask her mother for a rest, they emerged into a sparsely forested clearing. Stella could see the tall chain-link fence. The top two feet of fence slanted inward, so the wolves wouldn't be able to climb over.

Mack was waiting near the pen's gate. He was wearing a dark turtleneck under his parks department uniform. A baseball cap was pulled snugly down on his head.

"Norma," he said in greeting. "Hi there, Stella. You're up late."

"Hi." Stella felt shy around Mack. She wasn't sure how he'd feel about her being there—and she didn't want to get her mom in any trouble.

She stuck her hands in her pockets and looked around. Eight aluminum boxes had been placed at intervals inside the pen. The fenced-in land looked much like the surrounding countryside. Several trees grew inside.

Stella noticed a dead elk, which was just this side of the fence. She took a step away from it—not wanting to get a noseful of the stinking flesh. In the car, Norma had told Stella that her co-workers had dragged an elk bull that had been killed in a car accident up to the pen. It was to be the wolves' dinner. The wolves would have eaten the same sort of thing at home in Canada.

*Yum, yum,* Stella thought—her stomach turning over. She wondered if the wolves would really eat meat they hadn't caught themselves. Coyotes would. Then again, coyotes would eat almost anything. With luck, they would find out soon whether wolves were pickier eaters.

Norma moved toward the gate. "Well, they've been in those boxes for almost thirty-eight hours. Let's see if they're still alive."

Stella watched as Mack and her mom moved into the pen. Working swiftly, they slid up the door of each case and secured it. Stella expected the wolves to dash out immediately. But nothing happened. The cases were so still they could have been empty.

When all of the boxes were open, Norma and Mack came out of the pen. Pulling on gloves, Norma grabbed the elk's two hind hooves. Mack got the front. With effort, they dragged the elk across the ground and into the pen.

Mack exited quickly. But Norma lingered a moment longer in the pen. She approached each case one by one, peering inside and moving on. When she had finished her round, she came out and locked the gate.

"Let's get out of here," Mack whispered impatiently.

Stella was unsatisfied. "But how do we know the wolves are okay? Shouldn't they have come out?"

Mack and Norma exchanged uncertain looks. Norma pulled off her gloves, considering.

"I think it's a good sign," she said, stowing the gloves back in her pocket. "I would have been worried if the wolves had bounded right out of their cages. That would have suggested they are too trustful of humans. A little caution on their part is a positive thing."

"But they've been in those cases a long time," Stella argued. "Maybe they're sick—or dead."

Norma put a reassuring hand on Stella's head. "Well, they're not dead. Each one is scrunching way up in the back of its case like it's trying to hide."

"From us," Mack said forcefully. "The sooner we get our human scent out of here, the sooner they'll be able to relax. Jeffries will be here at dawn to check up on them."

Norma nodded. "Okay, my little pup, head out."

Part of Stella longed to stick around. She wanted to make sure the wolves were okay. And she wanted to be there to witness the moment one stepped out of its case, assuming one did.

"Come on, muffin, march." Norma nudged her and Stella headed toward the woods. At the edge, she turned back for one last look.

"Mom!" Stella whispered.

Norma and Mack turned back, and froze. The very tip of a furry snout was poking out of the case nearest them. Stella was only about ten feet away, and in the moonlight she could see the wolf's whiskers moving as he sniffed the pine-scented air.

Stella held her breath as one enormous paw tentatively reached out and touched the ground. Then another paw. Now Stella could see the densely furred face of the wolf. His wary golden eyes gleamed in the dark. His erect ears twitched nervously front and back.

"Gorgeous," Norma breathed.

"It's about time," Mack put in.

Stella shivered, and goose bumps rose up on her arms. Fifty years had passed since the last time a wolf walked in Goldenrock. She reached up and pulled on her mom's jacket. "Come on," she said. "Let's give them some peace."

## • 9 •

The threesome were quiet on their hike back through the woods. Stella was filled with a sense of great satisfaction. Something good had happened that night. Something right. And she'd been there to witness it.

Still, Stella was relieved to climb back into Norma's truck. And she felt even better crawling back into her bed. Her clock said 4:42. *I've got to get up soon and take Rufus out,* Stella thought.

The next thing she knew, the clock said 9:44. She sat up with a start. Poor Rufus! He must be dying to get outside. Stella jumped out of bed and rushed down to the kitchen.

She found her parents sitting at the kitchen table, drinking coffee.

"Hi, muffin, you're finally up," Jack greeted her.

Stella went to stand next to her mom. "Where's Rufus?"

"Cora is walking him," Norma explained.

"Did he go inside?" Stella asked.

"Oh, yeah." Norma laughed. "I had a little cleaning to do before I made coffee this morning."

Stella groaned. "Sometimes I think he's never going to get it."

Norma patted her back. "He's just a little puppy with a little bladder. He may not be able to hold it all night. Give him time."

"Run upstairs and get dressed, muffin," Jack said. "We're going out to breakfast to celebrate your mom's homecoming."

"Great idea!" Stella said. She loved eating breakfast out.

As soon as Stella was ready, the family piled into Norma's truck and made the short drive into town. They squeezed into the last parking spot at The Wooden Spoon, a diner in town. Jack bought a newspaper from a box out front.

Mrs. Crouse, one of the waitresses, led them to an empty table. She brought them water, silverware, and menus they didn't need to look at.

After a very short wait, Stella was tucking into a Breakfast Special: a thimbleful of orange juice, two scrambled eggs, hash browns, and bacon.

Norma tossed back her orange juice in one gulp. "So do you kids have anything planned for today? I was hoping we could spend some time together."

Spending the day with her mother sounded great to Stella. "I'm available."

"Me, too," Cora agreed. "Except I kind of promised May I'd see her at the goat show."

"The illustrious Fainting Goat Association's national show?" Jack asked.

Cora smiled. "The one and only."

Stella dipped a forkful of hashed browns into a pool of ketchup. "What's a fainting goat?"

"I have no clue," Norma admitted.

"I do," Cora said. "May told me all about it. Her cousin has a goat entered in the show."

"A fainting goat?" Jack asked.

"What else?" Cora said. "It's a fainting goat show."

"What's a fainting goat?" Stella asked again.

"I'm getting to that." Cora piled a big gob of egg onto her toast and bit it off. "Fainting goats are a special breed. They have something wrong with them that makes them freeze up when they're scared."

"Probably a genetic defect," Norma said.

"Whatever." Cora shrugged and reached for the jam. "Sheep farmers used to keep fainting goats with their flocks. If something threatened the sheep, like a coyote—"

"Or a wolf," Stella put in.

"Right," Cora agreed. "Anyway, the goat would

get scared and faint. Then the coyote would gobble up the goat, and the sheep would have time to escape."

Stella put down her fork. "That's disgusting."

"That's history," Cora said. "Nowadays most people just keep fainting goats as pets."

"That sounds like a must-see," Norma said.

Jack nodded. "I'm there."

Stella finished eating a few minutes later. She was ready to go. But her parents seemed to linger over their coffee *forever*.

Mrs. Crouse cleared their table.

Norma and Jack still didn't budge.

Cora sat slumped forward, her cheek resting in her palm, her eyes rolled toward the ceiling.

A bunch of people came over to welcome Norma back to town and exchange the latest gossip about the wolves. Stella learned that Mr. Jeffries, one of Norma's coworkers, had called that morning. He'd spied on the wolves at dawn. All of them had come out of their traveling cases. And the elk carcass had been partly gnawed. Clearly, the wolves were not sick.

Stella heard a muffled bleeping coming from her mother's jacket pocket. She dragged out the portable phone and flipped it open. "Hello?"

"Stella? It's Anya. I've been trying you guys at home all morning. Where are you?"

"Hi, Aunt Anya. We're at The Wooden Spoon.

We've been here for hours, and"—Stella shot her mother a meaningful look—"boy, am I bored!"

Anya laughed. "Just wait until you get old, kiddo. You'll slow down, too. Listen, I wanted to know how things went last night."

Stella gave her aunt a quick rundown on Stumpy—and the wolves.

"How's Queenie?" Stella asked.

"Much better," Anya said. "Maybe just a little depressed. She ate a good breakfast. I'm thinking of letting the Martins pick her up this afternoon. Or, since she has a long ride home, maybe tomorrow morning."

Stella felt a stab of disappointment. She was glad Queenie was doing better. But she had been looking forward to getting to know the dog better—and Devon, too.

"I have an idea!" Stella looked at her mother as she spoke into the phone. "Why don't we have Queenie and the Martins over for dinner tonight?"

Norma considered for a moment. "Why not? We have enough chili in the fridge to feed an army. Okay with you, Jack?"

"Sure."

"It's a go!" Stella told Anya. "Will you invite them when they come to visit Queenie?"

"Absolutely."

By then, Norma and Jack had finally had enough coffee.

Jack groaned and rubbed his belly as they waited on line to pay. "I could use a little exercise after that breakfast."

"Let's go for a hike down to the river," Norma suggested.

"Good idea," Jack said. "We can take lunch."

"I thought you wanted to *exercise*," Stella said.

"Exercise and then eat," Jack confirmed. When he got to the front of the line, he asked Mrs. Crouse to pack four box lunches. As soon as the lunches were ready and the bill paid, everyone climbed back in the truck.

"Are you tired, muffin?" Norma asked Stella as they buckled up.

"No way!" Stella said.

The goat show was being held at the county fairgrounds, about ten miles outside town. Norma turned down a road and drove under a banner that read TWELFTH ANNUAL FAINTING GOAT ASSOCIATION NATIONAL SHOW.

After Norma parked, the Sullivans wandered into the low barn buildings. Stella paused at the first stall. A goat stood in the middle of the stall, staring out at her.

Cora stopped next to her. She read a card that had been tacked up on the wall next to the stall. "Angela from Dubois, Wyoming."

"Looks like a normal goat," Jack commented. "Except maybe around the eyes."

The goat took a few steps closer, as if to say

hello. He was about two feet tall—slightly smaller than a run-of-the-mill goat. He had a short red coat. His eyes bulged out like a Boston terrier's. He had very long ears that stood out to the sides of his head.

"Boo!" Cora said.

"What are you doing?" Norma reached for Cora's arm.

Cora smiled impishly. "I was trying to scare him. I want to see him faint."

"Well, cut it out," Norma said.

Cora shrugged. They continued down the line of stalls, peeking in at the various animals. The color of their coats varied—black, tan, red, brown, gray, white. Some of the animals were rather scraggly-looking. Others were plump.

A lot of the owners were hanging out in the stalls with their animals. They seemed nervous. Judging was about to begin.

About halfway down the line of stalls, the Sullivans came across Cora's friend, May. She sat on a stool just inside a stall, looking bored. Another teenage girl was trying to tie an oversize red bow around a black-and-white goat's neck.

May's eyes lit up when she saw Cora. "Hey— you made it!"

"How's it going?" Cora responded.

The Sullivans gathered around the front of the stall.

"That's my cousin, Starr," May said, pointing

at the other girl. "Starr, this is my friend Cora and her family—Norma, Jack, and Stella."

May was a member of Kids for Pups. She'd sung a song about wolves at the rally Cora and Stella had organized.

Starr looked a bit like May—blond hair, brown eyes, and slightly too-big teeth.

"Hi!" Starr came forward and shook hands all around. "Nice to meet you folks. And I'd also like you to meet Hermy." She took the goat by his collar and dragged him forward.

Hermy was slender, with a gleaming coat and a mischievous glint in his eye.

"Pretty," Norma said.

Starr beamed. "Isn't he, though? Hermy comes from prizewinning stock. We live in Vermont, but my dad drove halfway across the country to buy Hermy from a top breeder in Wyoming. Fainters are very rare, you know."

"No, I didn't know that," Norma admitted.

"Oh, yes. There are only a few thousand in the whole country. This is Hermy's first show, but I'm positive the judges will be impressed!"

"Do you guys want to look around with us?" Cora offered.

"Yes!" May's face flooded with relief. She began to climb over the stall's wooden railing.

Starr looked doubtful. "Well, I don't know. The judging is about to begin. I wouldn't want to leave Hermy alone. Maybe I should just stay here and keep him company."

"Fine," May agreed immediately. "See you later!"

As soon as the group strolled out of Starr's earshot, May let out an exasperated groan. "Starr is driving me mad! All she's done since she got here is brag about what a great goat Hermy is. If I have to talk about that goat for another second, I'm going to scream!"

"It's just for one weekend," Cora said.

"Yeah. Forty-eight hours of torture."

"Have you seen Hermy faint?" Stella asked.

May made a skeptical face. "Starr says he's a

'premium' goat, which is supposed to mean he's a really dramatic fainter. But I think it's all a big joke. I've spent twenty-four hours with him, and he hasn't fainted once!"

Stella, for one, was glad that Hermy didn't pass out often. But a small part of her *was* disappointed. She wouldn't have minded seeing him faint once.

The Sullivans spent another twenty minutes at the show. They sampled some goat cheese, fingered a few mohair sweaters, and oohed and ahed over a litter of adorable baby goats.

"Well, I'm ready for lunch," Jack said.

"First we have to hike down to the river," Stella reminded him.

"Let's get going then."

They strolled back to Hermy's stall to say goodbye to Starr. Over Hermy's name card hung an enormous blue ribbon that said BEST OF SHOW in gold letters.

Starr looked prouder than the hen who laid golden eggs. "We won! We won!" she crowed.

"Oh great," May whispered in a low voice. "Now she actually has something to brag about."

# • 10 •

By the time the Sullivans emerged from the goat show, it was almost noon. With the sun high overhead, the temperature had soared into the fifties. The sky was a cobalt blue and completely cloudless.

Stella took a deep breath and sighed with contentment. What a beautiful day.

Jack took the wheel this time. He rolled down the windows and turned up the radio. As he drove, he sang and drummed his hand against the outside of the door. They passed under the arch into Gateway. The little parking lot at the trailhead was crammed with cars. Jack had to ease the truck onto the shoulder and park there.

Stella climbed out of the truck, pulling off her sweatshirt. She considered leaving the garment in the truck, but then decided against it. She knew the temperature would be lower near the water and under the shade of the trees.

Norma stuffed the box lunches into her day pack along with a couple of quarts of water.

They stopped to read the sign going in. "It's .8 miles to the riverbank," Jack read. "In other words, .8 miles until lunch."

Like Norma, Jack hiked quickly. He set off down the well-worn path that sloped gently toward the river.

Stella had to trot to keep up. Still, she was having fun—hopping over roots that grew across the path, being careful not to lose her footing on loose rocks.

Before long, the Sullivans caught up with a pair of hikers who were covering ground much more slowly.

Stella recognized Liv Stiller even from behind.

Liv was a grade ahead of Stella at John Colter Elementary. She was easy to identify because all of her clothes were blue, white, or blue and white. That day she was wearing navy leggings with a baby blue turtleneck. Even her dark hair seemed to have picked up a bluish cast.

Liv was with her mother—who was dressed in a variety of colors.

Cora and Jack called hello to Liv and her mother. But they didn't stop to talk. Norma fell into step with Liv's mom.

Stella caught up with Liv, and slowed her pace.

"Hi, Stella!" Liv said. "Check out my new dog."

Stella didn't see a dog. For a moment, she thought Liv was teasing her. But then Liv put two fingers between her lips and let out a piercing whistle.

A small dog came bounding through the underbrush. She ran to Liv and stood staring up at her, head cocked. The little dog seemed to be saying, "You called?"

Stella giggled. The dog only came up to about her knee, so she bent down to pet her.

"What's her name?" Stella asked.

"Lady," Liv said proudly.

"Hello, Lady!" Stella gave the dog a vigorous rub on the head. Lady responded by panting with excitement and licking Stella right on the lips.

Stella rubbed her hand across her mouth and stood up. Something about Lady seemed familiar. The compact dog had a white muzzle. The rest of her short coat was black, tan, and white. Her brown eyes were gentle, and her ears hung down. Her legs were longer than a basset hound's—but only slightly. Her front paws turned out like a ballerina's. She had a straight tail that was almost long enough for her to trip over.

"What kind of dog is she?" Stella asked.

"A drever," Liv said. "They're from Sweden—just like my family. My grandfather who lived in Uppsala used to have one."

Now Stella remembered. There was a photo of a drever in her dog book. She remembered reading that drevers were used to hunt bears. The breed was famous for its daring and fearlessness, which was out of proportion to its size.

"Liv, I think you should keep Lady on a leash in the woods," Stella said as they began walking again.

"I like to let her run," Liv said with a shrug. "She has a lot of energy."

Stella felt a flash of anger. Liv obviously loved her pet, but she was careless about her well-being. Stella took a deep breath and tried to explain.

"Did you know drevers were bred to hunt bears?" Stella asked.

"Bears, hares, and foxes," Liv said. "The breeder told us that. But I'm not planning to hunt with Lady. We just got her as a pet."

"Yeah, but all dogs are natural hunters," Stella pointed out. "What if she attacked a wild animal? She might do some serious damage—or get hurt herself."

Liv laughed. "Don't worry, Stella. Lady is as gentle as can be. She's not going to attack anything."

As the girls walked, Stella tried to think of some way she could get Liv to listen. She was still pondering the problem when she and Liv came out of the woods at the river. Lady immediately began dashing about, her nose to the ground, following some delicious scent.

Mrs. Stiller had unpacked a fishing pole and was trying her luck just below an abandoned beaver dam. The dam was old—weather-bleached white logs tangled together with brush. Behind the dam, water pooled still and deep.

"Looks like your mom has a good fishing hole," Stella said. She doubted that Mrs. Stiller would catch anything, though. Fish usually don't bite much in the middle of the day.

"She's good at that," Liv agreed. "See you later."

"Bye!" Stella went to join her sister on a flat rock a few yards into the river. She carefully stone-hopped across the water.

A few other groups of people had gathered around the riverbank. Norma and Jack were helping an elderly man in a red windbreaker read his trail map.

Stella reached the rock and flopped down. She leaned back on her hands and tilted her face toward the sun. After the cool half-light of the woods, the sun's heat felt terrific.

"You hungry?" Cora asked. "The sandwiches are tasty."

"I'll eat in a minute." Stella untied her sweatshirt, balled it up, put it down on the stone, and stretched out. The sweatshirt made a comfortable pillow. Lulled by the sun and the bubbling sound of the river, Stella closed her eyes.

She was awakened by Lady's sharp, excited barking. She sat up in time to see the dog streak down the river's muddy bank and attack—what?

Whatever it was looked almost like a fish: slick, muscled, made to live in water. But this was no fish.

Stella scrambled to her feet as Lady dashed forward, nipped at the creature, and then dashed back. She was barking fiercely without stopping to breathe. The creature moved swiftly, gracefully, turning its head to keep the dog in sight.

Everyone on the river was watching.

"Lady! Lady, come here!" Liv shouted frantically.

Lady ignored her.

Now another one of the creatures came out of the river. This one was much larger, and Stella got a clear look.

Long, brown, with a glistening coat. A whiskered face with a prominent black nose, dark eyes, tiny ears. Four short legs with a long, fur-covered tail.

An otter! Stella was at once thrilled and horrified. She'd never seen a river otter before, and the sight was electrifying. But Stella didn't want to see her first otter like this.

The larger otter—which had to be the smaller one's mother—smashed into Lady's side. The dog fell and rolled. The juvenile otter scurried toward

a shallow hole in the muddy bank and pressed back, trying to hide.

With a vicious snarl, Lady bit into the mother otter's hide. Swiftly, the otter turned and bit Lady in the neck.

Stella could see that Lady was in trouble. The otter was fast. Again and again, she landed bites on the dog's face and neck. She seemed to be winning the fight.

"Liv! Help me!" Stella shouted, suddenly moving into action. "The otter is going to kill Lady!"

# • 11 •

Stella scrambled across the stones to the bank. She picked up a stick. Waving it, she ran at Lady and the otter, screaming at the top of her lungs.

The mother otter froze. She rolled her eyes nervously up at Stella, not moving. Lady growled, showing her teeth.

*Now what?* Stella wondered. She certainly didn't want to hit the otter. But she had to do something to break up the fight.

"Yaaaa!" Stella hollered like some kind of deranged cattle herder. Liv dashed up to Stella's side, waving a stick of her own and stomping her feet. "Go away!" she screamed, her face streaming with tears. "Please go away!"

Then Cora dashed up, waving her arms wildly.

The mother otter decided she was outnumbered. In a blink, she scurried to the river, dived in, and disappeared.

Liv dropped to her knees and tried to hug the bloody dog. But Lady had other plans. She wiggled away, trotted over to the half-hidden otter kit, and let out a menacing growl.

Without thinking, Stella grabbed Lady's collar with one hand. She slipped her other hand under the dog's belly and hoisted her away from the otter.

Lady snarled and struggled, trying to get away.

Half-expecting to be bitten, Stella spun around so Lady couldn't see the otter. She hugged the dog tightly, forcing her to calm down. When Lady stopped wiggling, Stella thrust her into Liv's arms. She didn't let go until the other girl had a firm grip.

"Hold her tight!"

Liv nodded.

By that time, Norma, Jack, and Mrs. Stiller had reached the bank.

Mrs. Stiller was shaking as she fastened a leash to Lady's collar.

The others watched as Norma gave the dog a quick once-over. "What a mess. This puppy needs to have her ear and shoulder stitched up. You're lucky she's alive."

Stella fidgeted as her mother told Liv how to control Lady's bleeding and gave Mrs. Stiller directions to Anya's clinic. She was relieved when the Stillers hurried off. She couldn't help but feel the whole awful scene was Liv's fault. If she'd kept Lady on a leash, the fight never would have happened.

Norma cautiously crawled toward the otter kit. "Stay back, girls. This little guy is scared to death. He'll bite you given half the chance. Ew— I think he's bleeding."

"Can't we do something to help him?" Stella asked.

"We can try." Norma rubbed her eyes, thinking. "Otters are high-strung and strong. I don't think transporting him without a sedative is safe."

"Where can we get some?" Stella asked.

"Well, I know there's some ketamine in the glove compartment. And I think my syringe pole is still in the flatbed from my trip—"

"I'll get it," Stella said, without waiting to hear more.

Norma nodded. "Go."

Stella took off toward the parking lot at a run. Now she was hiking uphill, and the going was more difficult. By the time she passed the Stillers, Stella was covered with a thin coating of sweat.

Even pushing hard, it took her almost ten minutes to reach the parking lot. She fought to catch her breath as she pulled open the truck's passenger-side door. Inside the glove compartment, Stella found the bright yellow lockbox that held the little bottles of sedative. She grabbed it and moved around to the flatbed.

Relief flooded over Stella when she caught sight of Norma's syringe pole nestled against the side of the flatbed. She pulled it out, closed up the truck, and headed right back to the trail.

The syringe pole was a six-foot-long aluminum pole with a syringe attached to the far end. Norma would use it to poke the syringe into the otter's muscles from a safe distance. The pole broke down into three sections, so it wasn't too difficult to carry.

The return trip was easier. Stella ran down the trail—passing lots of curious-looking hikers. She didn't stop running until she got close to her mother and the otter. Then she slowed down so she wouldn't frighten the wild critter.

"That was fast," Norma said, as she took the equipment.

Nothing much on the riverbank had changed. The otter had conveniently turned its head away from the people—exposing its rear end. Norma quickly assembled the syringe pole and poked the otter in the rump. It reacted by trying to press even farther into the tiny hole in the bank.

"We'll be able to move him in a few minutes," Norma said.

Cora fetched Stella's sweatshirt to use as a

sling. Norma gently rolled the otter kit into the center. She gathered the four edges together.

The Sullivans hiked quickly back to their truck, with Jack carrying the kit. Norma held the kit on her lap for the short ride to the clinic. She kept him wrapped up in the sweatshirt to make sure he wouldn't get a chance to bite her.

"I'm in here!" Anya shouted, as they came through the front door.

"How's Lady?" Stella called back.

Anya poked her head out of an exam room. "She had a close call. But I think a few hundred stitches and some antibiotics will do the trick. How about you guys? You okay? Nobody got bit?"

"Only the kit," Stella said sadly.

"Put him in there." Anya pointed across the hall.

Jack and Norma disappeared into the other exam room.

Cora hovered in the hallway. "I'll wait here," she said—looking sick.

Stella nodded, and followed her parents. She watched as her mother pulled on thick leather gloves and gently unwrapped the otter. He was limp.

Norma let out a nervous sigh. "I hope I didn't overdose him," she said.

Anya bustled in, washed her hands, and pulled on some gloves of her own.

"Aunt Anya, have you ever treated an otter before?" Stella asked fearfully.

"Sure—once."

Jack and Stella exchanged worried looks as Anya gently rolled the kit over like an oversize sausage.

"Well!" Anya exclaimed. "Will you look at that!"

Stella crept forward. "What?"

"This little guy's in pretty good shape," Anya said. "Lady got in only a few bites. We should be able to stitch him up in no time. He'll be ready to hit the river tomorrow."

"Cool!" Stella said, relieved. "Can I come with you when you let him go?"

"Sure," Anya agreed. "I'm going to need you to show me exactly where this battle took place. If we release him there, maybe his mom will be able to find him."

"Great!" Stella said. "I'll get a cage ready in the—"

Just then, Cora poked her head into the room. "Stella, Liv wants to talk to you."

Stella went out into the hallway.

Mrs. Stiller and Liv were waiting for her.

Liv was holding a heavily bandaged Lady. She looked embarrassed. "I just wanted to thank you," she said. "And, um, to tell you that I'm going to keep Lady on a leash from now on."

"We really learned a lesson," Mrs. Stiller put in.

Stella was happy to hear it. She gave them a big smile. "I'm glad!"

Norma and Stella helped Anya get the otter settled in the boarder room. He was the only boarder since the Martinses had picked Queenie up earlier that afternoon.

It was almost dinnertime when the group left the clinic and headed home to get dinner ready for their guests.

Jack was the first one in the door. He quickly backed out, bumping into Cora, Norma, Anya, and Stella, who were jammed together on the porch.

"Phew!"

Stella's heart sank. "Is it Rufus?"

Jack nodded. His face was all scrunched up.

"Did he go inside?"

"Big-time."

"I'll clean it up," Stella said.

Jack nodded. "I'll wait here."

Stella pinched her nose closed and rushed into the kitchen. She ignored the scampering puppy until the mess was cleaned up. Even after the offending pile was gone, the Sullivans' kitchen stank.

Jack left the door open until the air cleared.

Stella picked up Rufus and gave him a kiss on his adorable furry face. "Don't worry," she whispered to him. "I know you're going to get the idea eventually. And I'm going to help by waking up extra early tomorrow morning."

Norma was pulling dishes out of the cabinet. "Why don't you keep Rufus in his kennel while Queenie is here?"

"Do I have to?"

Norma put the stack of dishes down on the table. "I think it's a good idea. He might not like having another dog in the house."

"Okay," Stella agreed reluctantly. She put the puppy in his kennel. Rufus whimpered for a few seconds, then settled down.

Stella was helping put out the silverware when the doorbell rang. "I'll get it!"

She raced to the door and threw it open. Devon, Mr. Martins, and Queenie were standing on the front step. Mr. Martins was holding Queenie's leash. Her hind leg was bandaged, and she was holding it slightly off the ground. She was panting slightly and her head drooped a little as if she were sleepy.

Devon had his cane. He looked tired, too. In fact, so did Mr. Martins. Stella was glad they'd come over for dinner. They definitely needed some cheering up!

"Hi." Stella hesitated, not quite sure what she should do about Devon. Should she offer to show him to a chair—or would that be rude? Finally she stepped inside and opened the door wider.

"Come in. Um, sit wherever you like. Can I do anything to help?"

"No, we're fine," Mr. Martins said. "Dev, the couch looks comfy. How will that be?"

"Fine."

Mr. Martins led Devon to the couch. Queenie immediately collapsed at his feet. She let out a sigh and put her head down on her paws.

Cora and Jack came out from the kitchen. Stella had just finished introducing the Martins to her dad when Anya came in, wiping her hands on a dish towel.

"I hope you're hungry!" Anya said cheerfully. "I just whipped up a batch of my famous home-made blue cheese dressing." She knelt in front of Queenie. "How's my favorite patient?"

"She's acting weird," Devon spoke up. "Sort of bummed out."

"Hmmm." Anya ran her hands over Queenie's head and peered into her eyes. Queenie licked Anya's hand wearily.

"She's had a hard couple of days," Anya reminded Devon. "Injured dogs sometimes get depressed just like people do. She'll probably snap out of it on her own. But just to be on the safe side, why don't you bring her by the clinic in the morning? I'll give her another quick check before you hit the road."

"We don't need to trouble you on a Sunday," Mr. Martins said.

"No trouble," Anya said. "Better safe than sorry."

"Dinner is served!" Norma called from the kitchen.

The rest of the evening was fun, Stella thought. After they finished eating, Stella introduced Devon to Rufus. Then Cora took him into the den, and they listened to CDs for almost an hour.

By the time everyone gathered on the front porch to say good night, Mr. Martins and Devon were smiling. But Queenie, Stella noticed, was still hanging her head. She saw Anya watching the dog, too.

## • 12 •

The next morning, Stella got up early.
But not early enough.

Bleary-eyed, she cleaned up Rufus's mess. Then, still dressed in the sweats she'd worn to bed, she snapped on his leash and led him out the front door for a walk.

Rufus was wide-awake. He ran as far forward as his leash would allow, his tiny legs a blur of speed. Then, panting, he ran back to Stella. He stopped to sniff a tree, lifting his leg to leave a little scent behind, then darted off into the neighbor's yard.

Stella stumbled along after him. The sun had just come up. Aside from a noisy flock of starlings off in the aspens somewhere, the neighborhood was quiet.

.At the end of the block, Stella turned back toward home. She noticed a goat munching on the dried grass in her neighbor's yard.

The neighbors were Ken and Jan Barber. They had a bunch of pets, Stella knew. Two golden retrievers, Max and Martha, and an old tomcat named Flicker.

But they didn't own a goat. And yet, there was a goat standing in their yard. He raised his head and watched as Stella drew closer.

*I think I know that goat,* Stella thought. He had a black-and-white coat, and a naughty gleam in his eyes.

"Hermy?" Stella said. "Is that you?"

It *was* Hermy, Stella was sure. Creeping a little closer, she saw that he still had on the red bow that Starr had tied around his neck.

But what was Hermy doing in the Barbers' yard? He must have escaped!

Stella started to walk across the Barbers' grass toward Hermy. But the goat was too sly for that. For each step Stella took forward, Hermy took one back. He was watching Stella's every move and chewing at the same time.

While Stella debated what to do, Rufus jumped forward and let out a tiny puppy bark. "Yip! Yip!"

"Rufus, no!" Stella said.

Hermy froze. His bulging eyes seemed to stick out even further. His legs went stiff. Then, while Stella watched in horror, he toppled right over

on his back! He lay motionless with his feet sticking up in the air.

Rufus hunkered down, whimpering.

"Oh, no," Stella muttered as she reached down
and scooped up the terrified puppy. Something
was terribly wrong with Hermy. She needed help.

Stella fled back to her house. She burst
through the kitchen door, and found Cora in her
pajamas, talking on the phone. "Here comes
Stella now," Cora said when she saw her. "Let
me ask her."

Cora pulled the phone away from her ear.
"Stella, did you see Hermy? He chewed right

through the strap Starr used to tie him up. May's entire family has been up since dawn looking for him."

"I—I saw him." Stella swallowed hard. "He's in the Barbers' yard. But, I—well, Rufus—"

"Stella found him!" Cora said into the phone. "Come on over." She turned the phone off.

Tears were welling up in Stella's eyes. "Cora, Rufus barked at Hermy. And then I guess he— he had a heart attack or something."

"Who had a heart attack?" Norma walked into the kitchen, and headed straight toward the coffee maker.

"Hermy."

"The goat?" Norma wasn't very sharp until she had her coffee.

"Yes!"

"A heart attack." Norma headed over to the freezer to get out the coffee beans. When she turned back to Stella, she was smiling. "Muffin— isn't Hermy supposed to be a *fainting* goat?"

"Mom, this was no faint! His legs were sticking straight up in the air."

There was a rap on the back door.

Stella glanced up and saw May and Starr standing there. She rushed to the door and opened it. Poor Starr. She was going to be so upset when she saw how sick Hermy was.

"Hey, Stella," May greeted her. "We just wanted to say thanks."

"Thanks?"

"Sure," Starr said. "I would have just died if anything had happened to Hermy. After all, he is an award-winning goat!"

Stella leaned out of the door. And there was Hermy, calmly pulling up the grass in her backyard. This time, Stella felt like *she* might faint.

"But he collapsed," Stella said in disbelief. "His feet were sticking up in the air!"

"Really?" Starr didn't seem too concerned. "He must have fainted."

"He recovered that quickly?" Cora asked.

Starr shrugged. "Sure. The faints only last about thirty seconds. He'll be stiff for a while. But it's no biggie."

Stella was so relieved that she burst into laughter. "He really scared me! It was kind of cool."

May looked mad. "I can't believe I missed it."

"Come on, May," Starr said. "We need to get home. I don't want my award-winning goat to miss breakfast!"

May backed off the porch. "Torture," she whispered.

After Hermy left, Stella ate breakfast and biked into town. She rode right past the clinic and stopped at the bait shop, where she purchased a couple of dozen live mountain suckers.

"Aunt Anya!" Stella called as she walked into the clinic. "I brought the otter's breakfast! And I decided we should call him Ozzie. That's a good name for an otter, isn't it?"

"In here!" Anya called from one of the exam rooms. "Thanks," she added, as Stella came in. "I haven't had time to feed Ozzie yet this morning."

"Why? What's up?" Stella put the soggy bag down in the sink.

Anya sighed. "Oh, it's Queenie."

"Queenie?"

"She took a turn for the worse last night. When the Martinses brought her in this morning, she could hardly breathe. I took some chest X rays and turned up a diaphragmatic hernia."

"A what?"

Anya was assembling surgical instruments: clippers, Betadine, sterile cloths, gloves, tweezers, scalpels. "Basically a tear in her diaphragm—that's the muscle between her chest and tummy. The tear is allowing her stomach, liver, and spleen to push into her chest cavity. That's putting pressure on her lungs and making it hard for her to breathe."

"Is it serious?"

"You bet."

"Did the accident cause it?"

"Yeah."

Stella's good mood evaporated. "Who is going to help you with the surgery?"

"Thought I'd tackle it myself. Your mom is still beat from her trip. And Owens is off somewhere."
Pete Owens was the veterinarian in Chico Hot

Springs, the small town about twenty miles up the road. He and Anya sometimes worked together. He usually spent Sundays fishing.

"I could help," Stella offered.

"Well—all right. I sure could use a couple more hands. Start by feeding Ozzie. By the time you're finished, I should be ready to operate. You can assist."

"Okay." Stella retrieved her soggy bag of fish and headed for the boarder room. She was nervous about being Anya's assistant for *the* operation, and her hands felt clammy.

*Think about one thing at a time,* she told herself. She approached the otter's cage slowly, not wanting to frighten the jumpy critter.

Ozzie heard her coming and backed into the far corner of his plastic dog kennel. He stood on his hind legs and watched her warily. Kneeling, Stella put her sack on the concrete floor. She opened the cardboard container and grabbed one of the sluggish mountain suckers by the tail. She opened the kennel door and tossed in one of the blunt-nosed fish.

The fish lay on the kennel floor, working its gills. Ozzie moved forward without taking his eyes off Stella, grabbed the fish, chewed quickly, and swallowed.

"Good boy," Stella murmured. "You liked that, didn't you? And guess what? There's more."

She waited until Ozzie was back in his corner.

Then she put down another fish. Ozzie grabbed it just as eagerly. Stella gave him another. And another. She fed Ozzie half a dozen fish—then began to worry.

Would otters eat until they exploded, like gold-fish supposedly did? Better not risk it. Stella closed up the box of fish and popped them into the fridge so they'd stay fresh until the otter's lunch.

Then she left the otter alone. Stella knew that learning to trust people could be dangerous for Ozzie once he returned to the wild. Besides, she had to assist Anya with Queenie.

The thought of seeing the operation made Stella's mouth go dry. She took a deep breath and pushed into the operating room.

Anya was dressed in her surgical blues. She'd already done most of the prep work. She'd given Queenie a drug to make her sleep. The dog was lying on her back. Her belly was shaved and disinfected. The rest of her body was covered in sterile drapes.

"Okay, honey," Anya greeted her. "Your mom told me what a good job you did with the breathing when you guys gave Queenie CPR. So I'm going to put you in charge of her breathing now."

She showed Stella a canvas "rebreathing" bag that was attached to a tube that ran into Queenie's lungs. Stella's job was to squeeze the bag every ten seconds.

Stella began counting. *One, two, three, four, five,*

*six, seven, eight, nine, ten.* Squeeze. *One, two, three . . .*

Anya picked up a scalpel and unwrapped it. "Ready?" she asked.

Stella swallowed and nodded. She tried not to flinch as Anya made a cut down the middle of Queenie's belly. But as Anya made a second cut, Stella forgot about being nervous. Without thinking, she drew closer for a better look.

Anya glanced up at her and smiled. She seemed to understand the fascination Stella felt.

"We're in the abdominal cavity now," Anya murmured. "Almost there."

Stella felt almost dizzy with anticipation. A thousand questions buzzed through her mind. Mostly, she wanted to know if Queenie was going to be okay. But she forced herself to hold her tongue. She didn't want to ruin her aunt's concentration.

It grew so quiet Stella could hear the seconds clicking by on the wall clock. Her hands got tired. Then they went numb. Still Stella continued to count. *Eight, nine, ten.* Squeeze. She jumped with surprise when Anya suddenly exclaimed, "Finished!"

"Did it go okay?"

"It went great." Anya stepped back and peeled off her bloody gloves. "Thanks, Stella. You were a big help."

Stella felt a surge of pride. She didn't feel tired anymore. "You're welcome."

## • 13 •

Anya wanted to stay in the clinic to keep an eye on Queenie Sunday night. So she and Stella made plans to release Ozzie Monday afternoon. Stella invited Liv to come along.

"Are you sure he can't get out of there?" Liv asked as they hiked down to the river. The otter was busily trying to chew his way through the plastic kennel Anya was carrying him in.

"The kennel will hold until we get to the river," Anya said. "At least . . . as long as we don't take too long."

Liv led the way down the trail. They made record time.

"Stay on the bank, girls." Anya stone-stepped across the river until she got to the same flat rock Stella had napped on a few days earlier.

Anya put down the cage and opened the door. Ozzie didn't hesitate. He wiggled out of the cage, leaped across the rock, and dived into the water. Stella saw a dark flash. Then he was gone.

For the next few afternoons Stella rushed to the clinic as soon as school was over. Devon would be waiting. Together, they fed Queenie, cleaned her cage, and took her for a walk.

As Queenie recovered, Stella realized how well her name suited her. The dog had a regal bearing and a calm intelligence. The Lab never jumped around with excitement the way Rufus did. Instead she showed her pleasure with a quick wag of her tail.

When Stella arrived at the clinic on Thursday, a station wagon with Colorado plates was parked out front. She dashed up the steps and found Mr. Martins, Devon, Anya, and Queenie standing together in the waiting room.

Queenie was wearing her elaborate harness, and standing patiently at Devon's side. She still had a bandage on her upper leg, a scratch on her nose, and stitches on her belly. But Queenie looked strong and bright-eyed. Her coat gleamed and she held her head high.

"Hi."

"Hi, Stella," Anya replied. "You're just in time to say good-bye to Queenie and her family."

"You're leaving today?"

Mr. Martins nodded. "Now that Queenie is well enough to travel, we have to get back. Devon's already missed a lot of school."

"And I haven't seen my mom in five weeks," Devon added.

Stella felt weird. Part of her was happy things had worked out well for Queenie and Devon. But a bigger part was sad that Queenie was leaving. She wanted to give the dog a hug good-bye, but somehow that seemed wrong. Queenie was working.

Instead, Stella reached out to pet Queenie's smooth brown head. "Bye, girl."

"Thanks for taking care of her," Devon said. "And us."

"You're welcome," Anya replied.

"You too, Stella," Devon said. "Thanks for everything."

"No problem."

"Well, let's hit the road!" Mr. Martins said.

Devon groaned. "Dad! Was that supposed to be funny?"

Mr. Martins threw up his hands. "I try!"

Stella's chest ached as they walked to the clinic's front door. Queenie was limping slightly, but Devon didn't seem to mind. He confidently followed Queenie down the steps and onto the sidewalk.

"What a great dog," Anya said.

"Yeah." Stella started to feel good as she

watched Queenie jump into the Martins' back-seat. Only one thing was worrying her. . . .

"Watch out for squirrels!" Stella hollered.

Mr. Martins turned and waved. Then he got into the car and started it up. He pulled into traffic. A moment later, the station wagon was out of sight.

Stella headed home to walk Rufus. Her heart sank as she turned into the driveway. Both of her parents' trucks were gone—which meant they hadn't come home from work yet. Norma was usually home by now. But she'd been hiking up to the wolf pen every afternoon that week. So far, the wolves were doing well.

No sign of Cora's bike either—which wasn't surprising. She worked at the stable after school on Wednesdays.

Stella was the first one home. That meant no-body had walked Rufus since lunchtime. She parked her bike and hurried up the back steps, preparing herself for a mess.

Rufus was waiting for her just inside the kitchen door. He wagged his tail so vigorously that his whole back end wiggled. "Yip!"

"Hi, sweetie!" Stella scooped him up. She tucked him under her arm as she inspected the newspapers spread over the floor.

They were dry.

Stella looked down at Rufus, completely amazed.

Rufus met her gaze. He let out a low, urgent

whine. The meaning was clear. He had to go—now.

Stella rushed across the kitchen, threw open the door, and put the puppy down.

Rufus ran into the grass. Gratefully, he sank into a squat and let loose.

Stella was so proud, she thought she might burst. "Good dog, Rufus," she murmured.

# WOLVES IN THE WEST

The story you just read is fiction. But a real-life battle over wolves has raged in the Western United States for almost two centuries.

When Lewis and Clark explored the Yellowstone region in the early 1800s, the plains were alive with as many as 35,000 wolves.

They weren't popular animals. Many European settlers from that time came to North America bringing terrible stories about wolves, like the Big Bad Wolf in *Little Red Riding Hood*, that had more to do with scaring children into behaving than with the truth. These fables were passed down from one generation to the next and helped cast the wolf in the role of a devilish beast.

During the 1850s and 1860s, wolf fur became a popular fashion. Tens of thousands of wolves were killed for their pelts. Settlers in the West also hunted the wild populations of bison, elk, moose, antelope, bighorn sheep, and deer until few remained. The native wolves began killing sheep and cattle in the absence of their natural prey. To protect their livestock, government agencies, along with ranchers, exterminated wolves from the land. And as the land was logged, mined, and developed for human use, the wolves had fewer places to live.

By 1930, wolves were nearly extinct in the United States. Over the years 80,000 wolves were killed in the state of Montana alone.

Today, people have come to realize the important role that wolves play in nature. Wolves are significant predators in North America. They help control populations of big-game animals like bison, moose, and deer, which in turn helps to reduce the damage to vegetation caused by these animals.

Also, many people are attracted to the idea of making the West "wild" again. They wanted to bring back the one animal their ancestors had completely removed from the Yellowstone ecosystem.

For these reasons, many programs have been started to reintroduce wolves into certain regions in the United States. One major program began in Yellowstone National Park.

Efforts to restore wolves to Yellowstone date back more than 20 years. Wolves are currently listed under the Endangered Species Act. This law protects animals and plants in danger of becoming extinct and provides recovery plans for each endangered species. Minnesota, with more than 2,000 wolves, is the only region south of Canada with a major population of wolves.

The reintroduction program allows for wolves to be brought into Yellowstone and surrounding regions from Canada. Thirty-one Canadian wolves were released in Yellowstone during the winters of 1995 and 1996. They were joined by 10 wolf cubs that were orphaned in northwestern Montana. By late 1998, the population in Yellowstone had increased to 118 wolves and the central Idaho group had grown from 35 to 114 wolves. The program is considered one of the most successful wildlife reintroductions in the United States.

Yet many ranchers oppose the program because they feel the wolves are a threat to their livestock. Since the program began, some wolves have been shot by ranchers for killing livestock. Now, the battle has been taken to the courtroom. The American Farm Bureau Federation has sued the U.S. Fish and Wildlife Service for bringing the wolves back to Yellowstone, and they are using legal challenges to try to prevent the program from continuing.

On December 11, 1997, Judge William Downes, of the Wyoming Federal District Court, issued a ruling that the reintroduction was illegal and that the wolves should be removed from Yellowstone and central Idaho. Many conservation groups are still fighting to keep the wolves, and they are currently appealing Judge Downes's decision. Until the appeal is heard, the wolves will remain; however, it is expected that the controversy will continue.